MAYA

AND THE RETURN OF THE GODLINGS

BY

RENA BARRON

HOUGHTON MIFFLIN HARCOURT
BOSTON   NEW YORK

hmhbooks.com

The text was set in Adobe Garamond Pro.
Cover design by Andrea Miller
Interior design by Sharismar Rodriguez and Andrea Miller

Library of Congress Cataloging-in-Publication Data is on file.
ISBN: 9780358106326

Manufactured in the United States of America
1 2021
4500830236

To the future storytellers, never give up.
This book is dedicated to you

. . . and to my family.

ONE

GUARDIAN IN TRAINING

TRAINING TO BE a guardian was hard. Harder than when I forgot to do my math homework for a week straight and Ms. Vanderbilt dropped a pop quiz. Harder than when I had to dust the house from top to bottom and clean the basement. Even harder than corndog day in the school cafeteria, when I had to pick off the mushy cornbread . . . *ew*.

Sweat streaked down my forehead and stung my eyes as I stood in front of the tear in the veil in the middle of Daley Plaza. It was six o'clock in the morning on the first day back to school, and I hadn't even brushed my teeth yet. I had startled awake thirty minutes ago when my version of Spidey sense kicked in. Anytime a tear happened, there was a ripple in the fabric of space. If it was close enough, I could feel a tingling sensation across my forearms.

"Do you need help, Maya?" Papa asked. His voice rang out clear as a bell in the plaza. "It's okay to ask if you do."

"I've got this," I said through gritted teeth.

I drew my staff across the Picasso sculpture in the plaza, which looked like a donkey with a jagged slash in its chest. This tear was stubborn. Some tears healed by themselves like a scab growing over a wound, but others needed Papa or me to close them. It didn't matter how small or big it was. What mattered was the depth of the tear. Meaning: did it stretch all the way to the Dark? Those were the ones that couldn't fix themselves.

Last week, Papa and I closed a tear over a swamp in Florida. It wouldn't have been so bad if not for the alligator who thought I looked like a tasty snack. He'd tried to sneak up on us, but Papa waved his hand and put the gator to sleep.

A couple of weeks before that, we braved the crowds at Lollapalooza, a music festival in Grant Park, only a few blocks from here. When we arrived, two guys were about to swing a third guy into the tear in the veil, thinking that it was an illusion. We got there in time to save their friend, and as soon as we closed the tear, no one remembered it had been there.

That was the weird part. Outside of my friends and

some of the people in my neighborhood, no one really knew the veil existed. Sure, some humans had seen it, but they didn't know about the darkbringers, the Lord of Shadows, or the Dark. Ignorance was bliss, but not when there was a revenge-thirsty god out to destroy your world. I understood why the orishas wanted to keep the threat secret, but more tears in the veil cropped up every day. It was hard for Papa to keep up with them, even with my help. Did I mention that this guardian-in-training business was hard?

"Mama's going to skin both our hides if I don't get you back in time for school," Papa said, leaning against the Picasso. He had a black staff with symbols etched in white paint identical to my own—except his staff was taller.

I changed my tactics and moved my staff around the edges of the tear, making a wide arc. "If I'm going to be late, it might as well be because I'm saving the world."

No one else in the plaza could see the tear or feel the cool breeze that whipped out from its mouth. Papa had cast a veil over the black hole, so we'd look like two hapless tourists checking out the Picasso. It was the perfect cover when we had to close tears in big cities or crowded areas.

Of course, being a guardian of the veil wasn't without problems. Papa and I had almost died in the Dark, and it was all my fault.

I wished that I could forget the whole thing, but I thought about the Dark a lot. I had struggled to make a gateway in time to escape, and the Lord of Shadows had been hot on our trail. Not to mention that the bridge of god symbols in my gateway had collapsed beneath our feet. Instead of running, we, um, fell through the gateway, but we made it back home.

It wasn't my first gateway, but after the battle, my magic was depleted. My magic. I still couldn't believe it, even as heat crept across my skin and a faint blue light traveled down my arms to the staff. The blue light was a new thing.

Thankfully, the Lord of Shadows couldn't enter our world through a tear. The veil prevented anyone with immense magic from passing through from either side. Although we'd found out the hard way that darkbringers who had little magic could still cross over. Having sharp horns and barbed tails didn't count toward the magic quota.

There were only two ways the Lord of Shadows and his army could cross into the human world. One: through an ancient gateway. The orishas had to destroy the one at Comic-Con after I . . . um, accidentally revealed the location to the Lord of Shadows. Two: if the veil failed. That was why Papa and I had to work around the clock to patch up the holes.

Before there was a veil—some five hundred forty million years ago—the darkbringers were destroying humans by accident. We were still sea slugs at the time, crushed beneath their feet. At first, the veil didn't work well, and many darkbringers died. Eshu, the orisha of balance, fixed it so that the human world and the Dark could both flourish. But the Lord of Shadows wanted revenge against my father and the orishas for what they'd done. Scratch that: he *still* wanted revenge. That part hadn't changed.

"See? It's almost done," I said as the veil began to shrink. This was the eighth hole since we got back from the Dark. A month of training, and I still took forever and a day to close a tear when Papa could do it in seconds.

"Keep this up, baby girl, and you won't be a guardian-in-training for long," Papa said, beaming at me. "You'll be a full guardian before you know it . . ." Papa's voice cracked and trailed off. His eyebrows pinched together as sweat beaded on his forehead. When he caught me watching him, Papa smiled again, but it was a weak smile, one that held a secret.

"Are you okay, Papa?" I asked, ignoring the tear that hadn't fully closed yet. The Lord of Shadows had drained his powers in the Dark, and it was taking time for him to recover his strength.

Before he could answer, something whipped out of the tear and snatched my legs from underneath me. Not some thing . . . writhing shadows.

I hit the ground hard on my butt, and the staff spun out of my hand. It rolled outside of the bubble of illusion that Papa had cast around the tear. The staff collided with a leather shoe belonging to a man in a gray suit.

The man reached down to pick it up and frowned at the glowing symbols. "What the bleep?"

Okay, he didn't say "bleep," but Mama said that I better not even think of cursing.

"Maya!" Papa said, lunging for me, but his legs buckled, and he stumbled instead. He reached for the place between his chest and stomach, his face twisted in pain.

He was getting worse, but I couldn't think about that now. The shadows still had my ankles and were dragging me into the tear. I needed to act fast before the darkness completely swallowed up my legs, and the rest of me with them.

Magic tingled in my hands as I reached for my staff. I yanked it free of the man in the gray suit, and it flew back to me. I hadn't thought about doing it—it was instinct. I knew that it would come back.

"Did you see that?" the man asked, looking around him, but no one answered. This was Chicago, after all. Most of the time, when someone said or did something weird, people ignored them and kept walking.

Papa stepped into the mouth of the tear. His dark skin glowed silvery-white and pushed back the darkness. The shadows hissed as if they couldn't stand the light and let go of my legs. I whacked one with my staff before they fled back into the Dark.

My face burned with shame as I climbed to my feet.

How could I let that happen after all the times Papa said to be careful? I should've heard the shadows coming.

Papa stared into the Dark, not moving a muscle. His face was grim and sweaty. Come to think of it, I'd never seen him break a sweat. Ever. That would've been weird before I found out that he was a god, a celestial, an orisha. What my father was had many names.

"Papa?" I swallowed hard as a cold chill ran down my back. The noise from the pedestrians and the traffic faded away. Even the roar of the tear in the veil sounded muted as I caught sight of what had Papa's attention. Darkness without start or end, without shape, without form, stood on the other side of the tear. I froze in place too, not seeing anything, but I could sense him there. *The Lord of Shadows.* I imagined his purple and black ribbons writhing around him.

My heart slammed against my chest, and my palms were slick against the staff. His presence loomed over us like a storm cloud. All around the edges of the tear, the color drained from the world. The brown metal of the Picasso faded gray. The gray stone beneath our feet turned almost white. The veil wouldn't let the Lord of Shadows cross into our world, but that didn't stop me from being afraid.

He said something in Sekirian, which I'd learned was the celestials' first language—the language of the universe. The ground trembled beneath my feet as his songlike whispers filled the air. Papa answered him, and the whole plaza shook. People almost lost their balance, and everyone asked if it was an earthquake.

"What's he saying, Papa?" I asked, after swallowing hard.

"Nothing of importance," my father said, gritting his teeth. Then he nudged me away from the tear with a hand on my shoulder. "That's enough practice for today. It's time to go home and get ready for school."

"I haven't finished fixing the veil," I said, but I was thinking about the Lord of Shadows. This was the first time that I'd sensed him on the other side of the veil since we escaped the Dark, and it sent ice down my veins. Papa had taught me how to avoid the crossroads, so I didn't see the Lord of Shadows in my dreams anymore. That was a huge relief—nothing like falling asleep and facing an angry god with a grudge against your entire species.

"You'll have other tears to practice on later," Papa said.

I didn't miss how tense his voice was as his magic swiveled toward the tear and closed it in a split second. I wished that my godling magic worked that fast. I could close a tear on my own without the staff channeling my powers, but it took me too long. With the staff, I still was much slower than Papa. He once told me that he'd patched up 2,057 tears in one day, which seemed impossible to me. Papa sometimes exaggerated, but I was starting to believe him.

Papa had transported us to Daley Plaza by bending space, a handy little trick that I had yet to learn. Bending space was different from what happened when we opened gateways. Gateways were more like cutting a temporary path through existing space. But Papa said that bending space was something else altogether. It required finesse to rewrite the rules of physics.

I could open a gateway to get us home faster, but I hadn't mastered the art of disguising mine. I didn't think people would respond well to a roaring, giant black hole in the middle of downtown Chicago. It was way too early in the school year to incite panic.

Today was the first time Papa had been too tired to transport us back home, so we took the Orange line. He was breathing hard after we climbed up the steps to the train platform high above Lake Street. Here was the thing: Papa was not human, no matter how hard it was for me to wrap my mind around that. He didn't need to breathe or sweat. He shouldn't have been tired, not in the way humans or godlings got tired. He leaned against the railing overlooking the street below.

"There's something wrong with you, isn't there?" I asked as tears spilled down my cheeks.

Papa inhaled a deep breath, his big shoulders shaking. He didn't have to say anything. I saw the answer written on his face.

TWO

NO MORE SECRETS, EXCEPT ONE

B Y THE TIME the train circled the Loop on the elevated tracks downtown, Papa had started to feel better. He gave me a big smile as he stood up and stretched his back. I stood up too, resting my staff on my sneaker instead of the sticky floor. Like always, the train smelled worse than an old, dirty shoe.

Papa stepped close to the sliding double doors. We still had plenty of stops before we got to Ashland Avenue, then we'd have to take a bus home. I could feel the static in the air as his magic spread like a fine mist around us. He was bending space on the train in the middle of rush hour. I nodded my approval—breaking the rules of physics was much faster than taking a train—but I wished that I could do it for him so he could rest. Real Talk: Papa did not come to play.

Almost everyone on our car was looking at their phones, but no one would notice us. Here was the thing about magic: most people wouldn't see it even if it smacked them right on the forehead. The key word being *most*. Some humans could perceive magic, so we still had to be careful. I found out at the beginning of summer that you couldn't even catch it on camera.

"The next stop is Roosevelt," the train's recorded voice announced. "Doors open on the left at Roosevelt."

The space in front of us shifted. It was subtle at first, like a cool breeze against our faces, but everything looked the same. When Papa was trapped in the Dark, the Lord of Shadows had stopped him from connecting to the veil to return home. He could fight to keep himself alive there, but he couldn't open a gateway or create a portal.

According to Papa, bending space across great distances could damage the universe. You make one mistake, and *boom*, you've wiped out a moon or a whole solar system. That was why gateways were much less risky for traveling across worlds or dimensions. They created a temporary bridge without changing the fabric of the universe. But for short distances, he said it was more convenient to create a portal by bending two points in space. Before I understood the difference, I used to think that gateways and portals were the same. I was still learning so much and having a hard time keeping up.

"We can't have you late for school," Papa said as the train's double doors slid open at Roosevelt. A man moved to exit, but he walked to the other set of doors, ignoring the ones that Papa had commandeered for his portal. The people on the platform waiting to board frowned at the open doors and did the same. This was wacky. To everyone else, the doors were out of service.

"How do you make the outside of your portals an illusion like that without even trying hard?" I asked.

When we passed through the doors, the train and platform faded away. I had to blink a few times to wrap my head around it. Here was the other difference between gateways and portals. When Papa or I built a gateway, it always had god symbols to connect two places together. My gateways were giant black holes on the outside and a bridge of spinning god symbols on the inside. Papa's gateways looked different every single time. He made a gateway once that reminded me of one of those moving walkways at the airport. Another time, we floated across an ocean on hoverboards shimmering with god symbols. Portals might've been faster than gateways, but they were also far less fun. When Papa bent space to create a portal, there was no bridge and no travel time.

"How do you know that I wasn't trying hard?" Papa asked as we stepped from the train platform onto the sidewalk on Ashland Avenue. I jolted forward from the force of the portal, which felt a little like being stuffed into a giant slingshot and propelled through space. The trip had taken a few seconds.

"You make it look so easy," I said as a woman startled next to us. She clutched her purse tighter and rushed away, glancing over her shoulder the whole time. From the way the woman ran off in terror, I had an idea of what she was thinking. She saw a Black guy with long locs and likely thought he was going to snatch her purse. I shook my head and rolled my eyes.

It wasn't like I hadn't heard my neighbor LJ complain about it all the time. Anime-loving, master gamer, LJ. He was tall, Black, and what Mama called *stocky*. Never been in trouble a day in his life, according to her. People would switch sidewalks to avoid him. If they were walking a dog, they'd make sure to put it between them and him. Mama said that a lot of people judged others based on stereotypes portrayed in the media. *Think of it this way,* she'd said. *If you always see rabbits on TV eating carrots, then you'll think that all rabbits eat is carrots. Imagine when the stereotype is more harmful and the damage it could do.*

"You should know by now, Maya, that things aren't always what they appear," Papa said, distracting my thoughts. "It takes great effort to bend space in two exact points to reach the desired destination. It took me a millennium to learn how to do it without causing an undesirable outcome." Papa frowned as he squeezed his staff. He had a pained look in his eyes like he was thinking about the past. "We can't afford to make mistakes . . . not like the one I made with the darkbringers. Not a day goes by that I don't regret it."

I couldn't imagine what it would mean for me to make a mistake that big. For now, I wasn't messing around with bending space.

"Why didn't you take us straight home?" I said, quirking an eyebrow.

"Earlier, you asked if something was wrong with me," Papa said. He leaned his weight on his staff as we walked down the sidewalk toward the corner store. "I told you before no more secrets between us, so I thought we should make a quick stop. We still have a little time before school starts." Papa let out a frustrated breath. "Truth is, baby girl, I don't know what's wrong with me, but Eshu might. He's got a unique ability to suss out ailments."

Eshu, the orisha of balance, sat on a red plastic crate in front of the corner store, playing his harmonica. He blew out a down-on-your-luck tune. You know the kind. A song that made you want to turn out your pockets to show the bully demanding your lunch money how broke you were.

The orisha tapped his foot along with the beat, and I couldn't see his harmonica lost in his brushy white beard. When Papa and I reached him, Eshu or I should say Ernest, which was his human disguise, stopped playing. His dark eyes glistened with flames that I was pretty sure no one else around saw.

Eshu frowned at Papa. "You don't look well, Eddy."

"I don't feel myself," Papa said, wiping sweat from his forehead.

"Your equilibrium is off." Eshu squinted at him. "That much I can see."

"What does that mean?" I asked, speaking out of turn.

"Hello to you too, young guardian," Eshu said like he was just noticing me standing there. He flashed a smile, and his eyes were smothered embers in pits of ashes. "Everything in the universe has equilibrium. Light and dark, matter and antimatter. Every creation, whether mortal or immortal."

Eshu had been the one to balance the veil so both the Dark and the human world could thrive. "Can't you fix Papa?"

"Maya," Papa warned, and I ducked my head.

"No, she's right, Eddy," Eshu said, rubbing his chin. "I should be able to sense why your equilibrium is off, but I can't. That has never happened before."

"The Lord of Shadows drained some of my powers, old friend," Papa said, brushing off Eshu's concern. "It's just taking longer for me to heal."

I thought about how the Lord of Shadows' writhing ribbons had hung Papa upside down in the Dark. His skin had turned gray, and then the Lord of Shadows tossed Papa aside like he was a broken toy. I swallowed hard and clenched my teeth. Next time I faced him, I'd be ready.

"Have you considered going to see Obatala in Azur?" Eshu asked. "He is the oldest among us and the wisest. He will be able to see what's wrong with you."

I had thought the mythical city in the clouds wasn't real. Papa used to tell me that people in Azur ate ice cream for breakfast and commuted to work on dragons. That Obatala, the orisha who helped create the darkbringers, lived there was a shock too. How could he be up there while the veil was failing here?

"I have . . ." Papa mumbled.

"And there's still the matter of the veil," Eshu said, almost apologetically.

I bit my tongue. If I were better at closing the tears on my own, Papa wouldn't have to work so hard. He could rest and get his full strength back.

"I can't figure out how the Lord of Shadows is causing the tears," Papa said. "For now, we're lucky he still can't cross into the human world, but the veil won't last much longer if he keeps damaging it." Papa pitched his voice low and grumbled under his breath. "If only I could create a new one, then we wouldn't be in this mess."

I glanced down at my sneakers, feeling sorry for Papa. He'd given up a part of himself to create the veil and a parallel world on earth. It wasn't something you could do every day, or even twice in an endless lifetime.

"Don't be so hard on yourself," Eshu said. "You've done everything that you could to protect this world. It was inevitable that the Lord of Shadows would find a way to start another war. What I don't understand is why he hasn't sent more darkbringers who can cross into our world. What's he waiting for?"

"He's got something bigger up his sleeve," Papa answered with no doubt in his voice. "He's lost against us twice and doesn't intend to lose again."

"The more reason for you to get healthy, brother," Eshu said. "We need you if things get worse. Go see Obatala."

When we left Eshu, I worked up my nerves to ask, "Can I come to Azur with you?"

"Yes." Papa nodded. "It's important as the guardian in training . . ." He paused, nudging my chin. "It's important as my daughter and the guardian in training that you know what's going on in case . . ." His voice cracked and trailed off.

"In case what?" I asked, a chill running down my back.

"Never mind that right now," Papa said. "Let's see what Sky Father says before we start speculating what might happen."

"When do we leave?" I asked excitedly.

"Tomorrow morning bright and early," Papa answered, still leaning on his staff.

I wasn't sure if that meant I'd have to miss school, but I decided not to ask in case he changed his mind. Papa getting better was way more important than the second day of school anyway.

"I need to rest and talk to Mama first," Papa said. "I'll ask Nana if Eli can go, and talk to Pam and Dee about Frankie coming, too. Best if you three stick together."

When we walked into the house, Mama was stirring in the kitchen, and the smell of bacon and eggs filled the air. She'd been asleep when Papa and I left to fix the veil. If it weren't the first day of school, she'd have been in bed until noon. Mama was still on the night shift at Stroger Hospital.

"Morning, Mama," I said as she walked into the living room with an apron over her red-and-white polka-dot pajamas. "You're up early."

"I could say the same for you." Mama gave Papa the Look (trademark)—the one that said they would have something to talk about later. "Now that school's started again, it's back to your regular schedule, okay? No more chasing tears at all hours of the night. You can help your father after school once your math tutoring and homework's done."

"But I'm never done with homework until dinnertime," I said, annoyed. "I won't have time to help Papa."

"I'm sure you two will find a way to make it work," Mama said. "Now, hurry up before you're late for school."

If we didn't keep patching up the veil, there wouldn't be any school. The darkbringers would destroy it along with everyone else. It wasn't like Mama didn't know that, but she liked to remind me that being a godling didn't exempt me from the rules.

"Maya, honey," Mama called after me as I ran upstairs to get ready. "Ms. Vanderbilt sent me an email this morning to remind you not to forget to turn in your math workbook today."

I froze at the top of the stairs. The same workbook that I hadn't finished yet. The one that had a dozen sketches of the warrior goddess Oya in the margins. It was only the first day of school, and my math teacher was already on my case. Typical.

THREE

I GO TOE-TO-TOE WITH A BULLY

I STUFFED MY HALF-FINISHED MATH WORKBOOK in my new backpack. Well, it wasn't *new* new. Mama got it used on eBay, but it was a limited-edition Oya backpack that came out a year ago. My school uniform, a white shirt and blue pants, clashed with the bag. It had nine strips of different colors across the front. Nine was Oya's favorite number. My favorite number was four, a number you could count on one hand and still have a finger left to spare.

I jetted downstairs, inhaled breakfast, and headed to Eli's house. The cranky Johnston twins, who lived next door, were out and prowling the sidewalk already.

"Try to behave yourself, Maya," Miss Ida said, leaning on her cane. She didn't need it. It was a cover to make people think she and her sister were two innocent old ladies.

They were old, way over the two-thousand-year mark, but they were also godlings like me. Miss Ida had saved me from writhing shadows one night. Miss Lucille had rescued Frankie, Eli, and me from a group of darkbringers in the park. Both had kicked darkbringer butt when the Lord of Shadows sent his cronies to rough up our neighborhood.

"Yes, ma'am," I replied, giving her a winning smile. "You too."

Miss Ida shook her head as if I was a lost cause, but Miss Lucille only huffed out a little laugh. She bent over their flower bed and pulled up weeds. I passed kids from Jackson Middle, messing around on their way to school. Priyanka was climbing into the back of her parents' SUV. Mr. Patel always dropped her off at school on his way to work.

I rang the bell at Eli's house, and the door creaked open. There was no one on the other side. "Um, hello?" I said to the empty hallway. Eli had discovered his godling power to turn invisible, which was golden for a kid who loved ghosts. He said that our neighborhood was haunted, but I had my doubts. The evidence was inconclusive. "Eli, stop messing around."

I jumped when I saw vines crawling across the floor, retreating away from me. I had no problem with moving vines, but in the half-light of the hallway, they looked like writhing shadows. I had a big problem with shadows, on account of them trying to kill me more than once.

"Come on in, Maya," Nana hollered from somewhere in the back of the house, then she raised her voice. "Eli should be ready!"

I kicked off my sneakers and walked into the living room. Nana had decorated it in brown, green, and orange for the fall. Vines inched along the walls like holiday lights.

"Maya, Maya, pants on fire!" Jayla, Eli's little sister, sang at the top of her lungs from upstairs.

"Stop jumping on my bed!" Eli groaned at her. "Go jump on yours."

"Jayla, get down here," Nana said, materializing in the living room.

I tried not to flinch a second time and failed. Nana Buruku, aka Nana, Mother Earth, stood in front of me in a white T-shirt and purple tights. She had a comb, a jar of hair butter, and a tub of barrettes in her arms. Eli's grandmother was the head of our local orisha council.

"How's training going, Maya?" she asked me as if she hadn't appeared out of thin air.

"It's going good," I said, not wanting to get into how Papa had to help me fix the tear this morning.

"I'm sure Elegguá could use the help," she said. "He's done it by himself for a long time."

Nana was right. Papa had been keeping the veil from failing forever, and I needed to be better with helping him.

It was too much work for one person with so many tears cropping up.

Jayla ran down the stairs giggling. She clutched something black in her hands and slipped behind Nana.

"Give me back my wave cap!" Eli said, hot on her trail.

A wave cap was a glorified headscarf for sleeping, so your hair looked good when you woke up. A lot of the boys at Jackson Middle wore them outside of school. By the time Jayla leaped from behind Nana, she'd crammed the cap on her head. It half covered her eyes, and she peeped from underneath it, smiling. "I'm like you now, Eli," she said, excited, puffs of her hair sticking from underneath the cap. She stroked her chin and tilted her head to the side, giving her best Eli impression.

Eli had looked annoyed when he first came down the stairs, but he grudgingly broke into a grin. "Since you're so inclined to mimic my handsome face, I guess you can keep it until I get back from school."

"I'm going to school, too," Jayla said, proudly. "Kindergarten."

"Not if you don't sit down and let me finish doing your hair," Nana said.

"I talked to Mom this morning," Eli said to his grandmother. "She said to tell you hi."

"How's she doing?" Nana asked, her voice softer than usual.

Eli exhaled a deep sigh. His parents had divorced after Jayla was born. His mother moved away, and his father, Nana's son, had decided he needed some space. "Good, I guess."

I didn't remember much about their parents, but Eli and Jayla had light skin and light eyes from their mom. Even when their parents had been around, they'd spent almost all of their time with Nana.

"Does your mom know about your powers?" I asked as we headed out the door on the way to meet Frankie.

"Nope, and neither does my dad." Eli tried to play it off like he didn't care, but he kept adjusting the straps on his backpack and glancing at his shoes. "I don't think my mom could handle it—she's got a lot going on. My dad will just say I'm making it up for attention."

Most godlings didn't show any powers, so they had no clue about their celestial family members. The orishas had kept their existence a secret, so I wasn't surprised that his father didn't know either.

Eli looked like he'd rather be talking about something else, so I blurted out, "Ugh, I'm not ready to go back to school. I didn't finish my homework from Ms. Vanderbilt."

"A crying shame, I tell you," Eli said, waving his arms around. "You should get a break for saving the world this summer with a lot of help from Frankie and yours truly." He flashed me a big smile as he pointed at himself.

"Couldn't have done it without you," I said, bumping my fist to his.

"Hey, don't forget that we have the kickball final after school," Eli said, changing the subject. "Don't be late again."

Ugh, I already *had* forgotten about it. I was definitely going to be late if I couldn't convince Ms. Vanderbilt to let me out of math tutoring.

When we arrived at Frankie's, her moms were debating whether life existed on other planets. Dee and Pam wore glasses almost identical to Frankie's yellow frames. The three of them had upgraded their glasses after Frankie got hers scratched up in the Dark. Dee was short and round, and Pam was tall and always wore big hoop earrings. Both of them worked at the University of Chicago. Dee was a scientist studying bacteria, and Pam was a biology professor.

"I'm not convinced that the radio waves CHIME picked up mean anything at all," Dee was saying as she opened the door. "More than likely, they're a naturally occurring phenomenon."

"Babe, you've got to be kidding," Pam said, shaking her head. "There is a clear pattern of intelligence that suggests life."

"Uh, sorry to interrupt, but is Frankie ready for school?" I asked, looking between the two. Pam was shoving books and a laptop into her leather messenger bag.

"Morning, Maya and Eli," Dee said, slipping into her

white lab coat. "Frankie's been up for hours—studying the properties of force fields in her room."

"Electromagnetic fields," Pam corrected in her teacher's know-it-all voice. "She thinks that *force fields* sounds too science fiction."

"Have you considered that all the science rules go out the window in the face of magic?" Eli asked, butting into their conversation.

Both Dee and Pam cocked their heads at Eli like he was proof that aliens did exist. They might've accepted gods and magic, but it didn't replace science in their eyes.

"Oh, you've got jokes early this morning," Dee said, laughing. "Good one."

Eli and I climbed up to the second floor to get Frankie. She was bending over a table, scribbling down notes. "Ready to go?" I asked, pausing at her open bedroom door.

"Almost," Frankie said, not looking up. "Come in."

Eli pushed into the room first and let out a long whistle. "It's nerd heaven up in here."

Entering Frankie's room was like walking into a laboratory. She had two desks—one with her laptop and one with her latest experiment. A box of beakers and test tubes sat in a corner by the door, near a pile of notepads she used to log her findings. But it wasn't all science stuff. Posters of her favorite bands were plastered on the walls, and she had a drool-worthy Lego collection.

Frankie stood in front of the desk with five jars of different sizes on it. Three of the jars were empty, but two of them sizzled with what looked like lightning. "I've been making electromagnetic fields all weekend. They seem to fluctuate in and out at random intervals before losing stability."

"You can keep them going without physical contact?" I said, picking up one of the jars. "That's a new trick." The lightning bounced off the glass like a Ping-Pong ball, sending a shock wave up my hand. I put the jar down fast, afraid that it might shatter. It was like the magic was desperate to free itself.

"Yes, but it takes a lot of concentration," Frankie said, biting her lip.

At least she was making progress. I wasn't any better at closing tears without my staff after weeks of practicing with Papa. I tried hard not to feel a little jealous, but I couldn't help it.

"I promised Nana that I would not get detention on the first day of school," Eli said. "We need to go before we're late."

"Right," Frankie said, reaching for her backpack. "I can't get in trouble again so soon after this summer. My parents only have so much patience."

Fifteen minutes later, we strolled through the front doors of Jackson Middle School. Even if I'd seen a lot of the same kids at the park this summer, everyone looked different in their school uniforms. Kids were sifting toward the crowded halls to find their friends.

"Welcome back to JMS, students," came Principal Ollie's smooth voice over the intercom. "We're looking forward to another exciting year!"

"Bulldogs, Bulldogs," a group of basketball players chanted as they pounded on the lockers.

JMS had so many sport teams and clubs, it was hard to keep up. We had the Bulldogs for basketball, the Jaguars for soccer, and the Bearcats for football. Baseball, swim, chess, robotics, drama, gymnastics. What we really needed was an official comic book club, that would be awesome.

"Hey, little Maya," Candace said, stepping in my path. "I see you forgot to grow this summer."

I swallowed hard and clenched my teeth. It was a well-known fact that Candace liked to pick her victims on the first day. She'd single you out, and then she'd be demanding your lunch money for the rest of the year. I might not have grown by much, but that didn't matter. I wasn't going to let her bully me.

"Hey, Candace," I said, ignoring the crowd of kids gathering around.

Instead of a snappy comeback, I decided to be what Mama called *diplomatic*. In addition to being one of Winston's cronies, Candace was a chess wizard and allegedly good at Ping-Pong. I figured it wouldn't hurt to give her a chance to talk about herself. "How was your summer? Win any chess tournaments?"

Every kid nearby cringed and the hallway fell silent. The fluorescent lights crackled over our heads. *Zap. Zap. Zap.* They might as well have been calling for a fight with the way today was playing out. I looked to Frankie and Eli, who both shrugged, not getting it either.

"Are you making fun of me?" Candace asked, her bottom lip trembling. I was close enough to see that her eyes had gotten all glossy.

"What happened?" someone whispered behind me.

"Didn't you hear?" someone answered. "A kid from the West Side beat Candace in three games straight. She ain't the chess queen no more."

Ugh, of course, I would pick the exact wrong thing to ask. "Uh, no," I said, scrambling for something else to say. "How's Ping-Pong?"

"Are you serious?" Candace growled, then she pitched her voice so everyone else could hear. "I sprained my wrist playing, and that's why I lost the chess tournament."

"What's a sprained wrist got to do with a game of strategy?" someone whispered, and Candace balled her hands into fists.

"I'm sorry to hear that," I said as I caught sight of something fishy going on with Candace's shoes. Her laces were untying themselves. "Eli!" I yelped.

"You think this is a joke," Candace said, taking one step forward. She stumbled over her feet and slammed straight into me. We both hit the floor hard.

Candace and I struggled to untangle ourselves in the middle of the hallway. Her elbow caught me in the ribs, and my knee connected with her side. She doubled over, her backpack slipping off her shoulder. It landed with a heavy thump next to my head. Two more inches to the left, and I would've been a cream puff. I wiggled from underneath her, my face hot from embarrassment. The first day of school was officially canceled.

"What do you have in there, a stack of bricks?" I groaned. The backpack was half open, and I saw, like, five books on chess. She was really taking her tournament loss this summer hard.

"Fight, fight, fight," kids yelled as Candace climbed to her feet.

She gritted her teeth, her lips squeezed tight together, and gave me her death stare. It felt like standing outside on a boiling-hot day or being an ant under a magnifying glass. The hallway had gone quiet again, and all eyes were on me. Sweat trickled down my back.

I got to my feet and squared up, shifting my legs to a wider stance and drawing my shoulders back. If Candace thought she was about to kick my butt, she had another thing coming. I didn't spend my summer fighting dark-bringers to be shown up on the first day of school by a bully.

Candace held out her hand, and Dion James, a kid with thick glasses, clambered forward to pick up her backpack. He shoved it into her arms with a little grin, and I could've sworn Candace blushed. "You're mighty clumsy, Maya," she said, her voice thundering in my ears. "I don't like clumsy people."

I caught a glimpse of Eli, who'd reappeared in the crowd next to Frankie. He mouthed a silent "Sorry."

The first homeroom bell rang, and to my surprise, Candace looked more relieved than me. Her big shoulders heaved up and down as she rolled her eyes. The death stare faded from her face like it'd all been an act. There was something different about her, but I couldn't put my finger on it.

"Saved by the bell," she said, turning on her heels.

"That didn't go at all how I expected," Eli said as the crowd broke up.

"You know if you bully Candace, that makes you as bad as her, right?" I groaned.

Eli shrugged. "She deserves to fall on her face every once in a while on account on how awful she is to everyone else."

"You're missing the point, Eli," I said, annoyed with him.

Frankie glanced around the hallway, oblivious to

our conversation. "Have you noticed that kids are acting strange?"

I thought about how the darkbringers had pretended to be some of our classmates earlier this summer. They'd been acting strange too before they showed their real faces. "Strange how?" I asked. "Like a little strange or a lot strange?"

Frankie pointed to a boy staring up at the ceiling as he walked. He kept bumping into other kids, who shoved him out of their way, but he didn't seem to notice.

"Why is everyone yelling?" asked a kid who had their hands shoved over their ears.

That was a weird thing to say because the kids who were usually the loudest in the hallway were extra quiet. Another kid was clutching his backpack like he thought someone would steal it.

"Get to homeroom, Ms. Abeola, Ms. Williams, and Mr. Flores," said our history teacher, Mr. Chang. He stood next to his classroom as the last of the students filed inside. "You don't want to start the school year on the wrong foot."

"As opposed to the right or left foot," Eli said under his breath before we parted ways.

Frankie was right, though. People were acting strange. I had a theory, but I didn't want to speculate, not until we saw more.

FOUR

THERE GOES THE NEIGHBORHOOD

THE REST OF THE SCHOOL DAY passed by in a blur. We attended a welcome assembly midmorning and got our schedules. Every year the seventh- and eighth-grade classes went on a joint field trip at the end of the first week. Principal Ollie announced that this year, we'd be going to the Field Museum.

After the last bell rang, I dreaded going to Ms. Vanderbilt with my half-finished workbook. I peeped my head in her classroom. She was in the middle of laying out quizzes on empty desks for tomorrow. A new kid I recognized from social studies sat in the front row, doodling. Her pencil scratched across her paper in long, furious strokes.

"Um, hello," I said.

Ms. Vanderbilt had her usual red 'fro pulled back into

a bushy ponytail. She glanced up and smiled. "Maya, have you met our transfer student, Gail Galanis, from upstate New York? She's going to be joining us for tutoring this year."

"Hi?" I said, not knowing why it came out as a question.

Gail yawned and slouched in her desk. "Hey."

"Nice work," Ms. Vanderbilt said, glancing over at Gail's paper. "You handled those pre-algebra questions like a pro."

I did a double take, staring at the drawing. Gail had arranged her answers together to create an unmistakable portrait of herself. Talk about retro selfies. But also, she was really good. My Oya sketches looked amateur compared to her work.

"Ms. Vanderbilt?" I asked, biting my lip. "Would it be okay to skip tutoring today?"

My math teacher shook her head like I'd asked her to stop the earth from spinning. "Skipping the first day of tutoring isn't a good start to the year, Maya, but if you must, so be it. Turn in your homework assignment, and I'll begin reviewing your answers."

"That's the other thing," I said, ducking my head. Ms. Vanderbilt pursed her lips, her eyes narrowing. "I need a few more days to finish it. I had a busy summer."

Ms. Vanderbilt sighed. "What could have possibly kept you from finishing your workbook for the entire summer?" She'd said it like summer was twelve years and a day long.

Um, saving the world, I almost said, but thought better of it. Ms. Vanderbilt wasn't an orisha or a godling, so she didn't know anything about the Dark or the Lord of Shadows. It was weird after everything that had happened to keep such a big secret. I didn't feel right about it, not since Papa said he wouldn't keep secrets from me about his job as the guardian of the veil. But he'd also said that humans would panic if they knew about the Dark.

Gail Galanis tilted her head to the side like she was waiting for me to answer Ms. Vanderbilt's question. I took her in for the first time. She was a little taller than me, with pale brown skin and dark eyes. She wore her black hair in a single braid that reached midway down her back. "I finished my workbook and only got it two weeks ago," she said, turning back to her drawing.

"Says the girl who doodled on her practice sheet," I said, crossing my arms.

"Maya, don't be rude," Ms. Vanderbilt said. "Please turn in your completed workbook by next Monday. That should give you plenty of time to finish it."

I looked back and forth between Ms. Vanderbilt and the new girl, annoyed. I didn't know Gail, but I already didn't trust her. No way she finished her whole workbook in two weeks on her own. She must have had help.

"Yes, ma'am," I said before rushing from the room. "See you tomorrow!"

I caught up with Eli and Frankie on the sidewalk in front of school.

"You're cutting it really close," Eli said, checking the time on his phone. "We need to hurry up, or we're going to be late for the game."

"Sorry," I grumbled as we set off for the park. "Ms. Vanderbilt insisted on introducing me to Gail Galanis— this new girl at school."

"She's in my homeroom," Frankie said, excitedly. "Artist type, always drawing."

"Yeah, *artist type*," I mumbled, rolling my eyes.

"Looks like you have some competition," Eli teased.

"Ugh," I groaned. The knot twisting in my belly was most definitely *not* jealousy.

"Get your mind right, fam," Eli said, tapping his temple. "We have a game to win."

The teams were still warming up when we made it to the park. People climbed the bleachers next to the field to get the best spot to see the game. Some stood in long lines in front of the hot dog and snow cone carts. Eli had convinced Frankie and me to join a kickball team when we got back from the Dark. He said it was a good way to stay in shape since we had to be on our A-game if the darkbringers ever got through the veil. Personally, I would've preferred lessons at the dojo.

"What the . . ." Eli said, cursing under his breath.

Winston, Tay, and Candace had lined up in our spots.

"Hey, Craig," I called to the team captain.

He straight up ignored me, so I called his name again. "CRAIG!"

"You're too late," he shot back, not even bothering to look at us.

"But the game hasn't started yet," Eli argued. "You're being completely unfair."

Winston shot me a smug smile over his shoulder. "Too bad."

I held my breath. The look on his face reminded me of the darkbringer who had pretended to be him earlier this summer. I almost thought that he was going to add "little godling" at the end of his sentence.

"Next time, you'll be begging us to play on your team," Eli said, glaring at Craig.

Frankie sighed, turning to go. "Come on."

We were almost off the field when someone screamed. The hairs stood up on the back of my neck as I whirled around. Kids scattered in every direction. Candace and Tay were backing away from Winston, who was on fire. Angry blue flames climbed up his arms.

"Argh!" he yelled as smoke curled around his body.

He was on fire, yes, but the flames weren't burning him.

I expected Winston's skin to turn deep purple or blue, or for him to sprout a barbed tail and wings. I grabbed for my staff, currently disguised as the butterfly clip in my hair. It shimmered with white light and grew into its full length right in front of everyone.

"I didn't sign up for this," Craig said, clutching the ball under his arm. He joined the rest of the crowd running away.

I brought the staff into a defensive position in front of me. "You picked the wrong day to mess with us, dark-bringer."

"What?" Winston asked, blinking back tears. "What's happening to me?" I almost felt sorry for him until he narrowed his eyes and flames shot straight for my head. "You did this!"

I ducked out of the way, and Winston looked quite pleased with himself.

"That's enough from both of you," Miss Ida said, stepping around me. The cranky twin wasn't wearing her pink bonnet. She had her silver hair in braids that swept down her back. She put a hand on Winston's shoulder and the flames across his skin sputtered once before they disappeared. I glanced around to see Miss Lucille, the other half of the cranky twins. Her blue magic spread across the entire park, stealing away people's memories.

I remembered what the orisha council told us about the godlings. Except for a couple, no godlings had shown powers for decades until Frankie, Eli, and me. But they also said that the last time before the war with the Dark, things had changed. . . It couldn't be — no way.

"He's a godling?" I asked, already knowing the answer before Miss Ida nodded once, a look of worry on her face.

"A bully turned godling," Eli proclaimed, throwing up his arms in defeat. "There goes the neighborhood!"

Winston was a bully with magical powers, but we were in bigger trouble than that. If more godlings were showing powers, the war with the Dark would come soon.

FIVE

I RIDE A HORSE MADE OF STARLIGHT

CANDACE AND TAY trailed behind as Miss Ida dragged Winston from the park like he was a lightweight. He twisted his arm and cursed but couldn't free himself from the cranky Johnston twin's grip. I knew what that felt like all too well after the night she rescued me from the writhing shadows.

"You better let me go, old lady," Winton demanded. "I'm not playing with you."

"Oh, you're not, eh?" Miss Ida said.

"I got all that on video." Tay grinned as he slipped his phone in his pocket. "My boy is about to go viral."

"That's what he thinks," Eli said, crossing his arm. "Winston finally does something worthy of the internet, and they have no proof of it."

"Serves him right for shooting fire at my head," I said, glaring at his back.

"He was wrong for that," Frankie added.

I remembered how the darkbringer pretending to be him had tried to kill me at the start of summer. How at Comic-Con, the fake Dr. Z had attempted to finish the job. And the countless times in the Dark when my friends and I came close to getting the ax. Now the biggest bully of our class could control fire—well, *not control it,* but he could call it up. It was just a matter of time before he'd learn how to use it and wreak even more havoc at school. This was very bad.

"The Johnston twins should lock that one up in a dungeon somewhere," Eli said, once they were out of earshot. "No way he's joining the League of Godlings."

Frankie sighed. "If he has powers, that can only mean one thing . . . and we might need his help."

"He's more likely to join the darkbringers than help us," I said, only half kidding. It was easier to make a joke instead of thinking about what this meant. With no way to stop the veil from failing, more godlings would show powers. The orisha council had told us that many godlings had died in the last war against the Dark. I didn't want to see that happen to anyone, not even Winston.

Within minutes, everything was back to normal in the park as if a kid hadn't just caught on fire. I glanced down at my feet, biting my lip. "Papa's sick," I said, finally getting it off my chest. "We're going to Azur to see if Obatala, the Sky Father, can figure out what's wrong with him."

"Is it even possible for a celestial to be sick?" Eli asked.

"Immortals aren't invincible," Frankie said, her voice low as she fiddled with her bracelet. The sunlight sparkled against the beads as she twisted them around her wrist. "Remember what Miss Lucille said about the Lord of Shadows absorbing the celestials . . . and my mom died."

I stopped in my tracks. Tears prickled in my eyes. Frankie still didn't know what happened to her first mom. Everyone said she went to the store to get milk and never came back, but there had to be more to it. Seeing my face, Frankie slapped her hand over her mouth, shaking her head.

"Maya, I'm sorry," she said. "I didn't mean to make it seem like . . ."

"It's all right—Papa is going to be okay," I said before she could finish her sentence. "Anyway, he's going to ask your families if you can come with us tomorrow morning before school. We're leaving extra early."

Eli grimaced. "Like *early* early?"

"Yup," I said, nodding.

"I'm in," Frankie said, flashing Eli a smile. She knew how much he hated getting up early.

"I better get home," I said, thinking about my math workbook. "See you in the morning!"

We executed a perfect three-way fist bump and parted ways. When I got home, Mama was next to Papa on the couch with her stethoscope pressed to his heart. She wore her usual scrubs: a pastel-colored flowered top and gray pants.

"You have an elevated heart rate." Mama's eyebrows knitted together in concentration. "I can't say what that means since you don't need your heart to live."

"How could I love you so much if I didn't have a heart?" Papa teased.

"I'm sure you'd find a way," Mama said, blushing. She drew the stethoscope back from his chest. "How do you feel now?"

"Like a million dollars," he answered with a winning smile.

"Why do you have to be so silly?" Mama grumbled, but she was smiling too. "This is serious."

To any other kid, this would sound like an odd conversation. Papa and the other orishas had human and semi-divine forms, but their true form was pure energy. That meant that he shouldn't be able to have a racing heartbeat or any physical ailments.

"Maya," Mama said, still looking at Papa, "make sure your father gets plenty of bed rest while I'm at work. No more patching up holes in the veil tonight."

"I will, Mama," I said, and I meant it. If we had another tear, I'd fix it myself, no matter how long it took.

"Dinner's on the stove," Mama said, coming to her feet.

I inhaled, taking in a whiff of tomato sauce and garlic and onion. Spaghetti. My stomach growled. Papa always made breakfast when he was home, and Mama made dinner. Things almost felt like they were normal again.

"How was your first day back at school, baby girl?" Papa asked.

I grimaced as I plopped down on the recliner. "Okay, I guess." I sucked in a deep breath. "Oh, Winston Turner burst into flames at the park."

"Another godling?" Mama said, her eyes meeting Papa's. They both looked worried.

Papa glanced down at his hands. "It's happening across the world in every sanctuary—more godlings showing powers."

Mama rubbed her forehead. "I'll call Destinee on my way to work. She isn't going to take the news about her son well, especially coming from Ida or Lucille."

"Are you coming with us to Azur tomorrow?" I asked Mama, then I realized I didn't know how that would work. "*Could* she come, Papa, even if she's not a godling?"

"If she wants," Papa said with a twinkle in his eyes. "But humans can only enter Azur with a celestial or godling to guide them."

Mama shook her head as the grandfather clock struck five. It was time for her to leave for her shift at the hospital.

"Oh, no, I can't get past the idea that the city is built on clouds . . . That doesn't help my fear of heights." She grabbed her purse from the table and kissed me on the forehead. "See that she doesn't eat too much ice cream, Eddy."

"Cross my heart," Papa said with a sly grin.

***

The next morning, Frankie and Eli showed up on our doorstep at seven o'clock sharp. Eli pulled off his wave cap and stuffed it into his backpack. He had indents across his forehead from wearing it. Frankie wore her retro green high-top sneakers to match her T-shirt, which read THINK LIKE A PROTON AND STAY POSITIVE.

Eli nodded at her shirt in appreciation. "That's actually pretty clever."

Both he and Frankie left their backpacks at my house as we headed out with Papa. I worried about what could happen while we were away in Azur. Even though the darkbringers hadn't been coming through the tears lately, they could. With so many new tears cropping up every day, it was sheer luck that most weren't stable. They could be waiting for us to leave to invade our neighborhood again.

"We're going to fly to Azur," Papa said, as sparks of his magic spiraled around us. "It's the best way to see the city."

"There's a plane that goes to Azur?" Frankie asked, frowning.

"Not exactly," Papa said. His magic started to take shape.

45

First a cluster of sparks here and another there. Then lines of light connected the sparks like a constellation of stars. Eli gasped as the magic settled into four winged horses. They stood side by side, their heads buried in the cranky twins' tulips, which they ate in big gulps.

"I don't think Miss Ida and Miss Lucille are going to be happy about that." I imagined the look on their faces when they discovered their tulips had become horse food.

"I'll make it up to them," Papa said as he grabbed the reins of the star horse closest to him. "You first, Maya," he said. "Show your friends how it's done."

I bit my lip. My only experience with horseback riding was the time we went to the Wisconsin State Fair. I got to ride one with a trainer standing on the side, guiding the horse in a slow circle.

"Um, Mr. Abeola," Eli said, his voice squeaky. "You do realize that we can see through these horses. There are gaps between the magic."

Papa grinned. "Nevertheless, Eli, the beasts are stable for flight. Trust me."

It was Frankie who took the reins of another starlight horse and climbed up first. She swung her legs across the back of the horse in one quick move like a pro. "I can confirm that it feels solid," she said as her horse lifted its head from the flowers and neighed.

"Feels solid isn't the same as *is* solid." Eli climbed onto his star horse. It bucked, lifting his front legs from the ground, and Eli yelped as he hugged himself against its neck. "Whoa now! This is not the time to be bouncing around."

As Papa helped me mount my horse, I saw LJ getting out of his car across the street in front of Lakesha's house. The two of them acted more like they were siblings than cousins. He waved at us, saying, "Nice bikes!"

"Is that what everyone else sees: bikes?" Frankie asked, her eyes wide.

"Of course!" I said, giddy with excitement. "The horses would look like something completely normal to human eyes."

"Mine is the dopest," Eli called to LJ, a grin on his face.

I resisted the urge to roll my eyes. Our horses looked exactly the same. LJ squinted, confused for a moment as he stared at Eli's horse. "Better keep it on lockdown—you know how it goes around here." He meant how, earlier this summer, a kid got his bike stolen by some teens from another neighborhood.

When LJ headed up to his cousin's house, Papa said, "Follow my lead."

He nudged his horse first, and it charged down the sidewalk. The horse leaped as its wings spread wide and took flight, soaring up and up. My heart was beating fast as I nudged my horse, too, harder than I intended. The horse bucked forward and took to the sky. My head spun a little, but I could feel magic all around me, holding me in place like a seat belt.

Papa left a trail of dust that spiraled upward as our neighborhood grew smaller. I glanced down at the tops of the buildings and cars that looked like ants. Soon we were in the clouds. The temperature started to change, but the magic adjusted to keep us warm.

"This isn't so bad," Eli yelled over the roar of the wind. "I think I'm getting the hang of this!"

It wasn't bad at all; in fact, it was really fun. The wind whipped through my locs like it was eager to carry us to Azur — like it was Oya's spirit. I never thought in a million years that I could be anywhere near as brave as she was in her comic books. She'd fought for justice against villains like Dr. Z until she set off on a quest fifty years ago. Papa said that it wasn't unusual for celestials to go on quests for centuries at a time.

I wondered what it would be like to travel across the universe fighting crime with the warrior goddess. Not that I would ever say that to Eli and Frankie. Hands down, they always had my back, and I wouldn't trade our friendship for anything.

Soon we were so high that we couldn't see the ground anymore. The star horses pumped their wings hard as Azur finally came into view. The city sat on a cloud that spanned for miles among the stars.

"Whoa," I whispered, stunned by the beauty of the city.

Papa slowed down his horse until we all four lined up to look at Azur from afar. Sunlight danced off the buildings made of silver and gold and glass. The whole city glowed. It was something out of a dream.

SIX

A CASE OF MISTAKEN IDENTITY

ZUR SAT ON A CLUSTER OF CLOUDS so thin around
the edges that you could see straight through
them. Smaller clouds surrounded the city like islands in an
ocean. In science class, we learned that clouds this high up
were made of tiny particles of ice. These clouds had to be
pure magic, or else there was no way they could support
thousands of buildings.

A palace straight out of a fairy tale stood in the center of everything. It had a dozen domed rooftops arranged
in a semicircle that shimmered in the sun. Was that where
Obatala lived? Miss Lucille had said that he was one of the
first celestials, along with Oduduwa, so he must be pretty
important. I hoped he could figure out what was wrong
with Papa.

"Are you three coming, or are you good with staring at the city from here?" Papa asked as he nudged his horse. It surged forward, star wings flapping in the breeze.

"Oh, we're coming," I said, as we set off after him again. I couldn't believe that this was happening. If someone had told me Azur was real four months ago, I would've said, *Quit playing*. Even though I was anxious for Obatala to help Papa, I was also excited about visiting the city for the first time.

We descended toward an empty courtyard, where a man stood waving two white flags. My horse neighed and changed directions. The other horses did the same, and soon we tapped down on the ground.

Eli hugged his horse around the neck. "Thanks for not dropping me." The horse huffed in annoyance.

The Azurian standing in front of us could almost have passed for human. He had pale skin and shaggy silvery hair, although the scales on his forehead and his neck were a dead giveaway. He grinned as his flags shrank in size, then he tucked a minuscule version of them into the pocket of his cargo pants. "Welcome back, old friend."

Papa beamed at him. "What are you doing on flight duty?"

The man shrugged with a crooked grin. "I accidentally turned Obatala's rose garden into a bed of vipers. I was trying to make them grow faster, but I used too much snake venom in my potion."

"Gavet, this is my baby girl, Maya," Papa introduced me, "and her friends Frankie and Eli."

"I'm not a baby, Papa," I said, under my breath.

Gavet propped his hands on his hips and looked at me with wide-eyed surprise. "Has it been so long that you have another child?"

A chill shot down my back. His words reminded me that Papa had a family before Mama. He had another wife and three children, Kimala, Genu, and Eleni. The Lord of Shadows didn't care that they were just kids. He killed them to hurt Papa, and he would do it again if he had the chance. Eleni had been only a year older than me, and Genu had been a little kid.

My brain hurt trying to keep all the problems straight in my head. The veil, the Lord of Shadows, and now Papa not feeling well.

"I wish that I could say that I'm here for a social visit," Papa said after a deep sigh. "I need to see Obatala."

Gavet squeezed the handle of one of the flags sticking out of his pocket like it was a nervous tic. "We heard the news about the veil. How bad is it?"

I bit my lip before I said something that would get me in trouble. It wasn't like the Azurians were in any danger from the Dark up here. They were safe. Well, scratch that — they were safe for now. The Lord of Shadows didn't strike me as the type to destroy earth and be satisfied. He'd want revenge against all orishas, including the ones who lived on Azur.

Papa cleared his throat. "If I recall, it's almost time for the autumn festival," he said, changing the subject. I got the feeling that he didn't want to say more about his reason for coming to Gavet. "The merchants must be starting to decorate the markets by now."

"You kids are in for a treat," Gavet said. How could both of them be so calm when all I wanted was to run to Obatala's palace? "I'll walk with you a bit. I'm due for a break."

Gavet fell into step beside Papa. They talked about football and a popular ice-skating competition on the rings of Saturn.

Eli glanced over his shoulders back at the star horses. Sparks of light lifted from their backs, scattering in the air like a tornado of dust bunnies. Soon the horses disappeared. "There go our rides home."

"That guy looks exactly like Gavet." Frankie squinted at a man standing on the field. He was waving his flag to direct a person flying on a giant hawk to land. He wore the same cargo pants and had the same shaggy silver hair.

"Maybe his twin?" I suggested, but somehow, I knew that wasn't true either. I looked around the field, and another Gavet was kneeling in a bed of roses. A third one was painting a mural of a cityscape on a fence.

"I see you've spotted my other selves," the Gavet with Papa called from behind us. "It's a handy trick, eh?"

"How many can you make?" Eli asked excitedly.

Gavet shrugged as we passed underneath a stone archway that led out of the courtyard. "Never tried more than a dozen or so. Didn't see the need to have more."

We walked alongside rows of rainbow tulips that would have put the cranky twins' flowers to shame. When a breeze swept through them, the air smelled like sugar and cinnamon and vanilla. I sucked in a deep breath, and Eli's stomach groaned. We passed by houses with paisley rooftops in every combination of colors imaginable. Orange and brown, yellow and purple, red and green, pink, gray, and black.

The Azurians were tall and lanky, short and plump, and every shape and size. Some had skin as smooth as marble or scales and gills like Gavet. Tails swept along the ground. Wings tucked against backs. Long tentacles wiggled among feet like a motorcycle dipping in and out of traffic. Papa had once told me that some of the Azurians were human — and I had a lot of questions about that.

"How are humans here if they aren't supposed to know about magic?" I asked.

"You're inquisitive, little one," said Gavet, laughing. "I see you're your father's daughter."

"She's got her Mama's sharp tongue and smarts," Papa said, and my chest swelled with pride. "To answer your question, Maya, the humans here all have the gift to see magic. It's a rare ability, but not unheard of. That's why we must always disguise our work with fixing the veil back home. Never can be too careful."

Eli wrinkled his nose at a pair of elokos who darted across our path. "Please tell me that those guys are vegetarians."

"Not quite," Gavet said, "but they've been weaned off human flesh."

"Until they get a craving," Eli said under his breath.

While we browsed the tables in the market, Papa got sidetracked by friends who hadn't seen him in centuries. Orange silk stretched from rooftop to rooftop, spreading out into a canopy across one street. It was so sheer that sunlight shimmered through it, casting the pavement in dancing stars. Groups of people walked by us eating anything from palm-size three-tiered cakes slathered in buttercream to wiggling black jellybeans to salad on a stick.

"Okay, this place must be heaven," Eli said, rubbing his belly. "I want to eat everything in sight." While he was craning his neck to eye everyone's food, I was drooling over the whiff of waffle cone filling my nose with pure joy.

"Zala, is that you?" asked a man who had stopped in our path. He eyed Frankie in disbelief. "I'd heard that . . .

that you'd . . ." His voice cracked like he was choking up, then he shook his head. He looked human on first appearance, with golden brown skin and dark eyes. He wore his hair in short twists that stuck up everywhere and a thick beard covered his cheeks. He reminded me of Wolverine from the X-Men. "Sorry, my mistake," he said, backing away. "I thought you were someone else."

The man whirled around to leave, and I almost jumped out of my skin. On the back of his head was another face covered in gray fur and brown spots. Dark eyes stared at us above a long black snout and sharp yellow teeth.

Eli whistled as he grabbed my shoulder. "That's a werehyena? Dannnng!"

"I'm not a werehyena, boy," snarled the man, um, hyena, taking a step closer to us. "You insult me again, and I'll take out one of your eyes."

"Hey, slow down," Eli said, backing away. "Honest mistake."

"You're a kishi," I said, speaking up.

Papa told me stories about the kishis. They had two faces—one human and one hyena. In his stories, they were always tricksters who literally had *two faces.* I had thought that he'd made that part up, like how sometimes people were two-faced. Meaning: you couldn't trust them with your secrets. Those were the sort of kids who would pretend to be your friend today and talk behind your back tomorrow. *The absolute worst.* At least people like Winston, Candace, and Tay didn't fake being your friend. You knew where they stood.

"What's it to you?" he said, baring his teeth at me.

I couldn't help but notice that his human side had been a lot calmer. His voice was different too. The hyena had a rough, grating voice like nails against a chalkboard.

"Did you know my orisha mother?" Frankie asked, getting over her shock in record time.

The hyena's big eyes went wide in surprise, then he frowned at Frankie, almost in suspicion. "Are you claiming to be Zala's daughter?" His deep growl softened, but not by much.

Frankie crossed her arms. "That's what I just said."

People moved around us, uneasy, as we stood facing the kishi. Papa and Gavet had gotten swallowed up by the crowd somewhere up ahead. The kishi's black lips stretched back, revealing his very large, very sharp teeth. He looked like he'd eat us if he thought he could get away with it. I fingered the silver coin in my pocket. Magic tingled through my hand, itching underneath my skin.

The kishi took one step toward us with his claws curled at his sides. "That's close enough," I said, pulling out the coin. It transformed back into a staff instantly.

"Did you know my mother or not?" Frankie demanded, her shoulders shaking.

The kishi spun around so that his human side faced us again. "I knew her," he said, finally accepting that Frankie was telling the truth. His voice was still deep, but his tone had turned regretful. "I lost track of Zala after she left Azur."

"My mom lived here?" Frankie asked, surprised by the news.

"Yes. Zala was the head peacekeeper for centuries in Azur," the kishi said. "She hunted down rogue magical creatures across the universe. Most were out to seed chaos or incite wars. She and I worked on many cases together. I considered her a friend."

Frankie bit her lip and asked in a daze, "What else can you tell me about my mom?"

"Zala went to earth after a rogue fugitive," the kishi continued. "After she completed the job, she settled there." He scratched his head, shifting on his heels. "She . . . um . . . fell in love with a human . . ." His voice trailed off like he was thinking hard about his next words. "I don't know what happened to your mother," the kishi said, "but celestials are not prone to accidents."

Frankie considered him for a moment, unable to speak. Silent tears slid down her cheeks, and I squeezed her shoulder to let her know that she wasn't alone. I felt helpless and didn't know what to say.

"My name is Charlie, by the way," the kishi said. "If you

need anything, give me a call. I owed your mother some favors, and by extension, I will grant them to you."

At that, he turned again, and his hyena face winked at us as he strolled off into the crowd. Could we trust the kishi, or was this a trick? It wouldn't make sense for him to lie about Frankie's mom.

"I knew it wasn't an accident," Frankie said, her voice full of defiance and anger. She pushed up her glasses that had slipped to the tip of her nose. "It never made sense to me, you know? Especially after I found out that she was a celestial."

I couldn't stop thinking about how the kishi—Charlie—told Frankie to call him but hadn't given his number. He had to know more than he was letting on. Worse than that, if Frankie's mom's death hadn't been an accident, that meant someone—or some*thing*—had killed her. We didn't know who or why, but we knew one thing for sure. The Lord of Shadows wasn't the only enemy in the universe powerful enough to kill a celestial.

I had a bad feeling that one day, we'd have to face this new enemy, too.

SEVEN

WHERE DO LOST SOULS GO?

FRANKIE RAN AFTER THE KISHI, but he disappeared into the crowd. When Eli and I caught up with her again, she was breathing hard. Her shoulders heaved up and down as she turned in a circle looking for him. We looked too, but the market had gotten busy fast. We ducked out of the way of an Azurian with four arms and eight tentacles balancing twelve spools of cloth. He was yelling at a group of people carrying baskets of gold fruit with little brown spikes to get out of his way.

"Where did he go?" Frankie said, her voice raw.

A knot balled up in my belly. Charlie said that Zala's death hadn't been an accident. I didn't blame Frankie for wanting to know what happened to her mom. "We'll find him again," I said, remembering how we'd used my staff to track down the gateway into the Dark.

An aziza boy with iridescent wings stuffed a powdered donut in his mouth as he ducked through the crowd. A woman with three eyes—two that wandered, one that stared straight ahead—pushed a cart past us. When she saw Eli gawking at her, she tossed him something that he caught in one hand. "Tell me my pixie-dust-infused mints aren't the best in Azur," the woman challenged him. "Come to Booth 479A and try some of my more exotic flavors. There's even one to fix your eye problem."

Eli's cheeks reddened as he rubbed the center of his fore-head, where her third eye had been. Then he unwrapped the candy and popped it in his mouth. Between smacking, he said, "It reminds me of rainbows and sunlight and picnics."

Frankie quirked an eyebrow at him, but I could tell that she was still thinking about the kishi.

"There you are," Papa said, waving for us to hurry up. Gavet wasn't with him anymore. "My favorite ice cream is up ahead. I thought we'd grab some before we head to see Obatala."

"Should we say something about Charlie?" I whispered to Frankie.

She shook her head. "Not until I get a chance to talk to him again first."

"I don't know, Frankie," Eli said. He wasn't smacking on the mint anymore, and his voice dropped low. "Can we really trust a man with two faces? You shouldn't get your hopes up."

"I have to find out if he knows more about what happened to my mom," Frankie said before we reached Papa.

Papa stood in front of a woman with pink hair in three buns stacked on top of each other like strawberry ice cream. "Long time no see, Guardian Elegguá," said the woman as she nodded to Papa. "Would you like the house special for you and your young charges?" The woman flashed a smile at me, and she had more platinum teeth than a rapper.

"You know it," Papa replied, grinning.

The woman opened the freezer in front of her and scooped up gray ice cream onto a waffle cone. Papa thanked her for his cone, and she fixed one for Frankie, Eli, and me.

"What flavor is it?" I asked, skeptical. I couldn't imagine any world where gray ice cream tasted good.

The woman quirked one eyebrow at me like I'd asked if the sky was up and the ground was down. Now that I thought about it, that was a complicated question for a city in the clouds. The sky was both up and down. "It's the house special."

"Oh, okay, thanks," I said before we set off again.

"So, who's going to try first?" Eli asked, but Papa had already started eating his ice cream.

Frankie took one lick from her cone and closed her eyes. She smiled as she tilted her head to the sky, and I could've sworn her brown skin soaked up the light itself. A single tear slid down her cheek. "It tastes like my mom's pecan pie."

When she said *mom,* I knew that she meant her orisha mom. I smiled too, happy that the ice cream had dug up a good memory, especially after the news from the kishi.

Eli sniffed his cone, and his jaw dropped. "Caramel popcorn."

"The ice cream will become any flavor you wish," Papa said, down two scoops already. "If you don't pick a flavor, then it'll pick for you. That's the fun part."

"Fun part, hmm," I said, giving it a try. At first, the ice cream tingled against my tongue. I smacked my lips a few times, and it tasted like a warm chocolate donut fresh out of the oven. "Mmmmm."

When we finished eating our ice cream, we headed out of the market. We passed outside the gates of the palace we'd seen from the sky. High hedges shielded the grounds from the public. "What's this place?" I asked Papa.

"The school," he answered as we walked across cobble-stones that looked like puddles of water. The way he said *the school* made me think it was the only one in Azur. I wondered what it would be like to go to a school where you didn't have to hide your magic. That had to be either fun or a complete disaster if there were bullies like Winston around.

We stopped at a little cottage on the edge of the city with shovels and rubber boots leaned against the beige walls. Brown straw covered the roof, and some of it blew away in the wind. From the outside, it didn't look like much —just a one-room shack—but I knew better than that. The gods were masters at making extraordinary things look mundane. Before Papa could knock, the door creaked open by itself.

"That's not creepy at all," Eli said. Frankie grumbled her agreement.

Papa seemed unfazed that we were staring into a pitch-black room. He stepped inside first, and we followed him. The door slammed shut behind us, and I squeezed my staff for reassurance—not that it helped. The symbols would usually glow under my touch, but they were dark here.

Torches on either side of the room flared to life. Their flames cast light on the dusty rug that led down a hallway. Our footsteps echoed as we walked, and I sensed the cottage was even bigger than the school.

"This place is weird," Eli said, louder than he should have, considering that Obatala had to be nearby.

"Sky Father has always been eccentric," Papa said.

Eccentric was a nice way of putting it. Obatala and Oduduwa made the darkbringers. Maybe if they hadn't, the

Lord of Shadows would've never crawled from behind his planet. Maybe I wouldn't exist either, because Papa would still be with his first family. I pushed that thought out of my mind.

"And you've always been quite the storyteller, little brother," came a voice from the shadows. "Eli, isn't it?" he said, addressing my friend. "Some call you weird for loving ghosts and the spirit world. You call it paranormal, but nothing in the universe is *not* normal. It's a work of art from the divine."

"How do you know that?" Eli asked, his cheeks bright with embarrassment.

"It's no more supernatural than atoms or energy or gravity," he answered. "All things that you believe in . . . Isn't that right, Frankie? Your hard science can never be disproved, except when it can . . ." He left that last point to hang in the air like it was a challenge for Frankie to try to prove him wrong.

"And, Maya, daughter of Elegguá, guardian of the veil in training," he said. I swallowed hard. "You claimed to have read every volume of *Oya: Warrior Goddess*. Yet there are three special-edition volumes in my possession that you haven't read."

"Really?" I said, almost forgetting the fact that this god knew way too much about us for my comfort. "So, you can . . . um . . . read minds or something?"

"Something like that," he answered as he swept out of the shadows. He was an older man in a white flowing robe with a trimmed beard, nothing like Eshu's brushy white one. He was much shorter than Papa, but not frail-looking for his age, with brown skin that shimmered with light. Miss Lucille had said that he'd been one of the universe's first children. That made him close to fourteen billion years old.

"It is good to see you again, Obatala," Papa said, bowing his head to the god, who returned the gesture with a big smile.

"I'm happy that you have come to visit, little brother," he answered. "And to meet Maya, Frankie, and Eli finally. There's been much talk about their antics on earth."

"Antics?" Eli grumbled under his breath. "We're heroes."

"I wish that I'd come under better circumstances," Papa said.

Obatala clasped his hands behind his back and walked alongside the torches. The flames flared up when he passed by them.

"It's no news to you by now that the veil is failing," Papa said. "I poured much of myself into its creation, and as much as I have tried, I can't make a new one."

"The veil is an extension of you, Elegguá," Obatala said, still pacing. "It has always been like a book on loan from a library that would eventually have to be returned."

Okay, that was a weird analogy, but I got what he was saying. When Papa made the veil, his magic split the earth into two halves — the human world and the Dark. And that part of himself would have to return one day.

"But that's not why the veil is failing, no," Obatala said, rubbing his chin.

"The Lord of Shadows has found a way to tap into its energy and drain it," Papa explained. "The same way that he killed so many of our kind."

Obatala stopped pacing, and then suddenly, in the span of a breath, he was standing in front of Papa. I had assumed his white hair and beard were from old age, but he looked younger than Papa. He had ice-white eyes that made me think he could, in fact, read my mind. If he could, then he'd know that his eyes really freaked me out.

"Are you always so squeamish, young guardian?" Obatala asked me.

I forced myself to look into his crystal eyes that formed a complex pattern. "No, Sky Father," I said, using the name that my father had.

"Good to know," Obatala said, smiling, "since your future is not for the faint of heart."

"You can see into the future too?" Eli interjected. Frankie nudged him in the side. When Obatala raised an eyebrow, Eli added, "Let me guess — 'something like that.'"

Instead of answering, Obatala turned to my father again.

"There is something wrong with you, brother. I sensed it the moment you reached Azur." He frowned.

"I haven't been myself since I got back from the Dark," Papa explained. "Eshu says that my balance is off, but he cannot see why."

Obatala's eyes began to glow, and the light from them filled the entire room. Out of reflex, I buried my face in the crook of my arm. The light was warm against my skin, but it also seemed to go straight through me. I felt weightless, almost like I could float away. When the light finally faded, I stumbled a bit. Frankie and Eli looked dazed and confused from it, too. Well, Eli looked confused *and* like he was itching to crack a joke, but he only rocked on his heels.

Obatala's eyes were wide with shock and fear. "A part of you is missing, little brother."

"What do you mean, missing?" I interrupted him.

Papa gave me one sharp look, and I bit my tongue.

"To put it in terms that you'll understand, young guardian," Obatala said. "His soul is gone."

My heart thundered against my chest. That couldn't be possible. Could it? Papa's face crumpled like balled-up paper, and his dark eyes looked hollow.

"When we were escaping the Dark, one of the Lord of Shadows' ribbons punched through my chest," he said, his voice low. "At the time, I felt a sharp pain, but I didn't think much of it."

"But can't Papa make a new soul?" I said, unable to keep quiet.

"For those of us born of the universe," Obatala said, "the essence of what we are is complicated. Our soul is our bond to the universe—it is our immortality. We cannot forge a new one."

"What are you saying?" I asked, tears streaking down my cheeks.

Obatala turned to my father to answer. "If you don't get your soul back from the Lord of Shadows, you will die." His voice rang in my ears over and over, along with the sound of my racing heart.

"No," I whispered. That couldn't be the only answer. Papa was too weak to go back into the Dark. He didn't stand a chance against the Lord of Shadows, especially not in his current condition.

EIGHT

I HASH OUT A PLAN

PAPA WRAPPED AN ARM around my shoulder and pulled me against his side. I sucked in a shaky breath that made my chest rattle. I wanted to bury my face and cry, but he was so quiet and calm that I had to be too. Both Eli and Frankie stood by, looking miserable. Frankie hugged her shoulders, and Eli shoved his hands in his jean pockets.

"This is your fault," I said, anger burning inside me. I glared at Obatala. "If you hadn't made the darkbringers and abandoned them, then the Lord of Shadows would have never woken up."

"Maya!" Papa said, my name sharp on his tongue.

"But it's true, Papa." I didn't care if I got in trouble for speaking up. It had to be said.

"The young guardian is right," Obatala sighed. Something warmed in his eyes, and for the first time since we arrived, he looked old. Not exactly millions of years old, but old enough to have regrets.

"I don't regret the darkbringers, but I regret not understanding the nature of life at the time. I'd like to think I speak for Oduduwa too. He thought that we could reason with the Lord of Shadows, but he was so very wrong."

Sky Father's voice was sad now, and his sadness filled the room like storm clouds threatening rain. It weighed down on us, and even Papa's calm face broke. I wiped away a fresh batch of tears from my cheeks.

"You asked me if I could see into the future," Obatala said as the overwhelming feeling of sadness lifted. "I can take a very educated guess based on the past and data in my possession, but the future is full of possibilities." He eyed me expectantly, and I thought I understood. He'd said that the road ahead of me would be challenging. Papa couldn't go back into the Dark, but I could.

"In any case," Obatala said, "the celestials from the edges of the universe should arrive soon. I estimate about three more months for the first ones to reach earth. Until then, Elegguá, you must preserve your life by not using your magic. When we do stand against the Dark, our priority will be to retrieve your soul and make you whole again."

"Three months?" Frankie grimaced and her nose wrinkled beneath her glasses. "How do you know that the veil won't fall before then? Tears have been happening exponentially . . ."

Eli cast Frankie a sidelong stare as if to say, *plain English, please.*

"Meaning that they've been occurring at an accelerated rate," Frankie continued without missing a beat. "What calculations did you do to conclude that the veil will last that long?"

Instead of answering her question, Obatala smiled. "I'm pleased to see that you're so much like Zala." Frankie hiccuped in surprise and covered her mouth, too stunned to talk. "Your mother never accepted anything at face value either."

"So," Eli interrupted, crossing his arms. "You're making another educated guess."

I stared Obatala straight in his ice-white eyes. "And you're guessing about Papa too, aren't you?"

"No," he said, his voice firm and far-reaching. His answer seemed to have many meanings. No, he wasn't guessing. Papa's soul was missing. He was dying. He couldn't use his magic anymore if he wanted to survive long enough for the others to arrive.

"I can't stand by while new tears form in the veil," Papa said, shifting heel to heel, his hands on his hips. He stared down at me, his long locs falling across his shoulders. "I might not be able to go back into the Dark, but the veil is my responsibility."

"If you keep using your magic, it will kill you," said Obatala, shaking his head.

No way. Not happening. "I'll fix the veil, Papa," I said, speaking up. "I'll do a better job so you can rest."

"Oh, baby girl," Papa said, kneeling in front of me. He took my hands into his own and squeezed. His eyes twinkled with pride. "You're already doing such a wonderful job."

"Go home and rest, little brother." Obatala waved a hand, and the air shifted around him. Papa climbed to his feet. "Let your daughter continue to help with the veil. Tell the council what has happened. If they agree to go into the Dark before the other celestials arrive, I will stand with them."

I cocked an eyebrow, wondering why he couldn't make them agree to go now. He was the oldest of the orishas and the most powerful. He shouldn't have to wait for them to make a decision, especially after what happened last time. They'd decided against going into the Dark to save Papa. They were too afraid of the Lord of Shadows. The cranky twins said that the councils called the shots on earth, but they'd listen to Obatala. Wouldn't they?

"You can take this path back home," Obatala said.

His magic felt heavy in the air again. It made it harder to breathe. The room started to shake, and I almost lost my footing.

"Azur is tethered to earth's atmosphere," Obatala explained. "When there is a significant tear in the veil, we can feel it here. Eventually, if the veil falls, the Lord of Shadows will come for us too."

My cheeks warmed at the news. I'd thought the Azurians were safe from the Lord of Shadows and his darkbringers for now. I shouldn't have jumped to conclusions without having all the facts. *It won't fall if I have anything to do with it.*

"I'm sorry I couldn't be more helpful, Elegguá," Obatala said as he clasped a hand on my father's shoulder. "Talk to the council and convince them to strike now."

Papa shook his head. "It's best if we wait until the others have arrived. We stand a better chance that way."

"I will, of course, respect their wishes," Obatala said.

"Let's go home," Papa said, gesturing to Eli, Frankie, and me.

We'd gotten the answer we came for, but it wasn't the answer we wanted to hear. It wasn't an answer that I could stand by and accept. I had to do something. I wasn't going to let the veil fail or let Papa die.

We stepped into a gateway of spinning god symbols. Like before, when I entered the crossroads of the gods' realm, I got the sense of endless doors to endless worlds. The Lord of Shadows could destroy them one by one. The fact that he'd stolen my father's soul made my skin burn with anger.

"A word, young guardian," Obatala said, appearing as shifting white smoke in the gateway. Papa and the others were up ahead and didn't seem to notice him. "You're planning to steal back your father's soul with or without the council's blessing, yes?"

I nodded without putting a voice to my answer. He sure was good at guessing for a god who claimed that he couldn't see the future. "Keep in mind that their magic binds everyone who swears an oath to the council. You cannot go against their wishes, even if you want to. Do you understand what I'm saying?" His ice-white eyes, the only solid thing about him, narrowed. The rest of him was white smoke spiraling in circles.

"Yes, I think so," I whispered back. When Papa was missing, no one went against the council to try to rescue him—maybe they couldn't. The cranky twins had been sworn to protect our family, and even they hadn't dared to defy the council.

"Keep that in mind when dealing with the council in the future," he said before his smoke began to melt away.

I squinted at the fading smoke until it was gone, and I jogged to catch up with Papa and my friends. Obatala had given me a valuable piece of advice, and I wouldn't forget what it meant.

The gateway put us smack in front of our house. Papa stared into the living room window, where we could see Mama pacing back and forth on the phone.

"Time for school." Papa inhaled a shaky breath, and something rattled in his chest. It was an emptiness that wasn't there before. "Be careful, Maya, and don't take any unnecessary risks."

"Wait a minute," Eli said, checking his phone. "Wait a dang minute."

"It's still morning here," Frankie said as two kids ran past us with their backpacks bouncing up and down.

"We've only been gone for five minutes," Eli confirmed. "Unbelievable."

"Time works a little differently on Azur," Papa said, shrugging. "Can't have you kids missing school."

When we were a block away from Jackson Middle, Eli looked to Frankie, who gave him a single nod. "Just so you know, Maya," he blurted out. "We're coming with you to rescue your father's soul."

I glanced between my friends, happy that they had my back. They hadn't even bothered talking it over. "It's going to be dangerous."

"It was dangerous the first time," Frankie remarked like

that was old news. "Now we're stronger, and we know what we're up against."

I told them what Obatala said about the orisha council. How if we pledged our loyalty to them, we couldn't go against their orders.

"Then we don't pledge," Eli said. "I get the feeling that they like to play by the rules, but we don't have to."

I pushed down a nervous grin as we bumped fists. I couldn't do this without them. "We're not the League of Godlings for nothing."

Eli winked at me. "The name is catching on."

I got that tingling feeling across my forearms again like a thousand ants marching on my skin. I had almost forgotten about the tear in the veil that had shaken the clouds in Azur. "Ugh, duty calls," I said. No way was I letting Papa take any unnecessary risks. "I have to go fix a tear in the veil. I'll be back before first period."

"We're coming with you," Frankie said. "Can't let you do this alone."

We stepped into an alley, and I drew the staff in a circle. Sparks crackled in the air, and a black hole rearranged garbage cans to make space for my gateway. "Let's get in and get out fast."

NINE

Rules are meant to be broken

After repairing the veil in California, I opened a gateway two blocks from school. We popped out behind the broken-down van in the vacant lot between two old buildings. The gateway closed within moments. At least I had gotten better at that over this summer. The trick was to start collapsing the other side as soon as we'd passed through it. I only wished that I could close a tear in the veil that fast. My staff shrank into a silver ring covered in god symbols, and I slipped it on my finger.

"Do you know what the staff will become before it changes?" Frankie asked.

"Not really." I shrugged. "It's a bit like the ice cream on Azur. I let my magic shape it."

"That's cool," Eli said, as we crossed the lot. "Check this

out." He held up his hand in front of his face. His fingers shimmered until his whole arm disappeared. "I've mastered making only parts of me invisible."

Frankie laughed. "Who knows when we'll need a dis-embodied body part to scare away our enemies."

The smile faded from Eli's face, and his arm turned solid again. "Not all of us can open doors into other dimensions or make force fields. It doesn't mean my powers aren't important."

Frankie nudged his shoulder. "I was joking."

"Sure," Eli groaned.

"You saved our butts twice in the Dark," I said to make him feel better. "If you hadn't stopped that helicopter—" I remembered the way the darkbringer helicopter, shaped like a giant bug, had burst into flames.

Eli's face had gone ghastly pale. "You think I wanted to bring that bugacopter down?" He glanced away. "I'm pretty sure the pilot didn't survive the fire."

"Sorry, I know . . . That's not what I meant." I swallowed hard, lost for words. We had to fight a lot of darkbringers to rescue my father, but the crash had been devastating. Papa said that sometimes we had to do things we weren't proud of. And even though I knew we had to stop the pilot to save ourselves, I still felt some kind of way over what happened. "Have you talked to Nana about it?"

Eli cleared his throat, making it a point to be extra loud.

"So, anyway, when are we going to save your father's soul so we can keep the veil from falling?" His eyes were shiny like wet marbles as he forced back tears. I wished that he would talk to Nana, but I understood why he wasn't ready. "I have to keep my little sister safe."

"We go today during gym," I said, biting my lip. "I don't want to wait."

Frankie gasped. "Without supplies? That's a terrible idea."

"We'll grab some stuff from the corner store," I said. "I have an emergency credit card."

Eli winked at me. "Commence Operation Go Dark."

"Excuse me?" I frowned as we detoured from our route to make a stop at the store.

"Operation Go Dark," he repeated as if it made more sense the second time. "That's going to be our code for getting into the Dark."

All through the walk to the store and on the way to school, Eli talked about the code names the Davis brothers used on *Ghost Sightings,* so I zoned out.

When we got to Jackson Middle, the street was busy with kids. Ogun, the god of war, was back in his usual disguise as our school crossing guard, Zane. He stood nearly seven feet tall, with a clean-shaven head and a neatly-trimmed goatee. He wore all green and combat boots. Even his dog, General, looked like a normal bloodhound, which meant that he was still twice my size.

"Oh, if it isn't Maya and her band of fools." Winston elbowed me in the side on the steps outside of the main building. "You're lucky that old lady saved you at the park."

Blood rushed to my head, and I leaped at him, but a hand clamped down on my shoulder. "Get to homeroom, Miss Abeola," Principal Ollie said, then they lowered their voice. "You need to set an example for the new godlings."

"He started it," I said, but Winston had slipped back into the crowd.

A couple of kids pushing each other caught Principal Ollie's attention. "I see you two are itching for a week of detention."

"Remember the plan," I told Frankie and Eli as the first bell rang.

I jetted off to my class down the hall and ran straight into a girl juggling a stack of books. She stumbled forward and tripped over her own feet. I tried to help her, but an identical girl stepped up and caught her arm. Twins. They had to be transfer students, since I'd never seen them before. "Sorry," I said as one of the twins glared at me. The girls were tall, with golden eyes and brown skin. They both wore their hair in braids pulled back into a ponytail.

"Nice move, Abeola," Gail Galanis said, flashing a temporary tattoo of a bear that covered her forearm. It would be my luck to have several classes with her.

"I see you're breaking dress code," I said, staring at her tattoo.

"Rules are meant to be broken," she said in a singsong voice.

Gail was trying too hard to act cool, and it showed. I was not looking forward to spending the whole year in after-school tutoring with her.

Aside from the incident with the twins, first and second periods flew by fast. I hurried back into the hall at the bell to catch up with Frankie and Eli. People leaned against lockers and chatted with their friends. Most of the new incoming sixth graders looked lost and confused. I was pushing my way through the crowd when I noticed several things at once. Eve Greyson, one of the popular kids, was crying next to the water fountain. "They grew on her face in first period," someone exclaimed. When I looked closer, I saw the problem. Eve had red, blistering pimples all over her cheeks and forehead.

Farther down the hallway, a boy I'd seen only a few days ago at the park stood two feet taller. Some mean kids were calling him the Green Giant. His arms and legs had ripped his clothes. Another girl was floating a few inches above the floor, screaming for someone to help her. The whole hallway was in an uproar. The teachers—the ones who weren't in shock—tried to get things under control.

Tisha Thomas stepped in my path. "What is the Dark?" She hadn't talked to me since last year, when she made fun of my stories about Papa. Now her eyes were glowing and glazed over as she stared at me. "What's the Dark?" she asked again, her voice like a robot. "You keep thinking about it."

I gasped, recognizing what was happening. More godlings were coming into their powers. A lot more. This was very bad.

"What are godlings?" Tisha asked as I pushed past her. I had to find Eli and Frankie.

I took off my ring, channeling my magic to reach out to my friends. Heat shot down my fingers, and static crackled in my ears.

"Hello?" Eli answered, his voice faded and distant.

"It's me," I said.

"How are you calling my phone?" he asked. "Instead of a number, I got a weird symbol."

"I can hear both of you through my earbuds," Frankie chimed in.

Instead of answering, I said, "This is our chance. Meet me in the Time Out room. This early in the day, it should still be empty."

"On it," they said.

A cloud of blue magic weaved through the hallway, and people screamed and started to panic even more. I pushed and shoved my way through the crowd until I reached the south stairs. I took them two at a time to the second floor. I was half out of breath when I entered the Time Out room.

Instead of regular time out, the school had replaced all the desks with yoga mats and medicine balls. Kids could try breathing exercises instead of going to detention. Eli and Frankie stood in the middle of the room, facing down one of the twins from earlier.

"What are you doing here?" I demanded, annoyed.

The twin crossed her arms. "I could ask you three the same, but I already know the answer."

As soon as I heard her husky voice, I cringed in horror. To everyone else's ears, she might have sounded like a normal twelve-year-old. But I knew that bossy tone.

"Miss Ida?" I shouted, my heart thundering against my chest.

"Yes, Maya," she shot back, turning her glare on me. "The council asked us to keep an eye on you at school."

"So, you turned yourselves into seventh graders?" Eli asked, quirking an eyebrow. "That's just wrong on so many levels."

"Ugh, that wasn't my idea!" she said, stomping her feet.

This was going to be much harder than I thought with the cranky twins at school now. "You're wasting your time, because we're here for meditation." I gestured at the yoga mats.

"Then I'll join you," Miss Ida said. It was weird looking at a girl my age and calling her Miss anything.

"Never mind," I groaned, turning to leave as Frankie

and Eli sidestepped her. "I don't feel like meditating any-more."

"Do you want some advice, Maya?" Miss Ida said.

"No, thank you." I rolled my eyes, although I didn't let her see me. Even if she looked like a kid right now, I still would get in trouble for back-talking my elders.

"Remember when my sister said that a godling let the Lord of Shadows into the human world the last time?" she said, ignoring me. "That godling used to disobey her parents too. She didn't follow the rules, and she thought she knew better than the adults around her. It got her killed."

I stopped cold and spun around. Miss Lucille had said that a godling opened a gateway into the Dark. That was how the Lord of Shadows attacked the human world. At the time, I didn't think much of it. How did I let that bit of information slide without questioning her further? A godling would need a key to open a gateway or would have to be a guardian in training.

"What are you saying?" I asked, barely able to get the words out.

"Your half sister Eleni opened the gateway and freed the Lord of Shadows," Miss Ida answered. Her every word was a knife with a sharp edge that cut deep. "It was an accident that got her, and so many others, killed. Don't make the same mistake."

TEN

THE ORISHA COUNCIL CALLS FOR A VOTE

FOR THE SECOND DAY in a row, I skipped after-school tutoring with Ms. Vanderbilt. I had one thing on my mind: the orisha council. My stomach balled up in a knot as I worried about how Mama had taken the news. If I knew Papa, he went straight to the council after talking to her—and I bet she'd gone with him. They should have taken me, too. It was time for everyone to start treating me like a guardian in training. How could I help protect our world from the Dark, when nobody trusted me to take risks and make hard decisions?

People swarmed the community center, enjoying the last days of summer. They crowded on the basketball courts and the playground. Kids lined up to check in for the pool, and a group of adults headed for the main hall, where Nana hosted bingo night.

Standing in the black-and-white-checkered lobby, I remembered the last time I was here. Papa was missing. Now things were much worse. The sense of uncertainty I had before was gone. I knew who I was up against this time, but that didn't mean I wasn't scared.

Carla, the godling receptionist, popped her head up from the video playing on her phone. She looked sixteen but was older than the cranky Johnston twins at two thousand and seventy-three. "I take it that you're not here for the pool party."

"We're here to see the council," I said, looking around to make sure that no one could overhear our conversation. The orisha council's headquarters was top secret. Only a third of the parents and children in our neighborhood were godlings—and most of them didn't know it. I still didn't agree that the gods should hide who they were from their human families. Well, scratch that. Many of them were about to find out after today's disaster at school.

Carla flipped through sheets of paper on a clipboard, scanning line by line. "I don't see your names on the guest list."

"Um, we must've been left off by accident," I said.

She glanced at her vibrating phone. "I'm not supposed to let kids up there without an adult accompanying them." She picked up the phone and frowned. "Ewww, who is this little twit commenting on all my old Instagram posts?"

Eli snickered next to me as he looked down at his empty palm. His thumbs moved up and down in a tapping motion. Was he doing what I thought? He'd turned his phone invisible and was trolling Clara.

"Umm, anyway," I said, clearing my throat. "We would've come with my father, but I was busy fixing a tear in the veil. You know, like, keeping everyone safe from the Lord of Shadows."

Carla's shoulders tensed as she glanced up again. "Right . . . sorry, did you say you were with your father?" Not waiting for me to answer, she waved her hand toward the metal detector. "Go on, then."

I was ready for the burst of force that pulled us through the metal detector. It sent us careening midair across the white room, which was a gateway between our world and the gods' realm. We stopped short of the giant doors and descended the three stories on an invisible elevator. My heart sped up, but I wasn't going to back down now.

We stepped through the doors into the gods' realm. It was like before—a place carved in outer space with no walls, no borders, except the endless stars. The orisha council sat on their thrones, looming in the chamber, larger than life. I would never get used to how majestic they appeared in their semidivine states.

"What a surprise that the three of you showed up without being summoned," Nana Buruku said.

Eli waved at his grandmother, his cheeks red. "Hi, Nana."

Nana was Mother Earth, and vines wriggled up the sides and back of her throne. Her white hair was braided in a ring around her head, and her skin glowed with light. To her left sat Shangó, aka Mr. Jenkins, Frankie's favorite science teacher. Lightning crackled above his throne. No surprise that he was the orisha of thunder and lightning. Next to him sat Eshu, with his bushy white beard. A fire burned at the center of his eyes, rimmed by blue ice. Among the orishas, he represented balance.

Next to him was Ogun, aka Zane, our crossing guard at school, the god of metal and war, and his six-eyed dog, General. Both wore matching metal tags that seemed to absorb the light from the stars. Ogun's face was unreadable as he stroked General's back like he was in deep thought.

To the far right was Oshun, the orisha of beauty, aka Miss Mae, who owned the salon on Forty-Seventh Street. Today she wore a gold dress that looked like it had stars woven into the fabric. Her makeup, like always, was flawless. Her throne was gold with peacock feathers fanned across the back that cast off the perfect light for a selfie.

Orishas, godlings, and humans alike filled the bleachers

across from the council. Their voices buzzed in the chamber as they argued with each other. From the sound of it, some of the human parents were pretty upset with their orisha family members. Mama and Papa sat on the bottom row, quiet. She smiled at me with sad eyes, and I wiped away a fresh batch of tears.

Frankie's moms, Dee and Pam, sat next to them. Jayla played with the other small children on a floating jungle gym off to the side. Winston, who was sitting with his mom, rolled his eyes when he saw us. I wasn't exactly happy to see him either.

Miss Lucille and Miss Ida had returned to their old selves and stood near the council. I recognized so many faces: Principal Ollie, Tay, Candace, Tisha Thomas, Eve Greyson. Some older godlings in their twenties and thirties were here, too. The clerk from the corner store. The ice cream truck driver. A cashier from the grocery store. The librarian.

"So the council summoned everyone except us?" I asked, biting back my annoyance.

"I voted against excluding you," Shangó said, a fierce look in his eyes. "But some people on the council outvoted me." He cut his eyes at Nana.

"These children have gone through enough," Oshun interrupted, batting her long lashes. "They have already risked their lives to save the world once. We cannot ask more of them."

"Truly, Oshun," said the god of war, "if they had listened to this council the first time, we'd be at war already. We owe them our thanks and gratitude."

The room had fallen quiet, and all eyes were on Frankie, Eli, and me. I ducked my head, feeling a little self-conscious. People usually didn't pay much attention to us. It didn't help that Eli couldn't have a conversation without bringing up ghosts. Frankie always had to prove that she was the smartest person in the room. And I'd been called teacher's pet for years because of after-school tutoring.

Eshu raised a hand to calm the bickering on the council. "They're here now, so let the young guardian and her friends listen to what we have to say along with everyone else."

Winston faked a cough. "Guardian of what? Giant turds?"

"Hush, boy," his mom said. "Now isn't the time for your smart mouth."

Winston slumped his back against the bleachers behind him, looking plenty embarrassed. I pursed my lips to hold back a smile. Served him right for always being so awful.

"Well, then, sit," Nana waved to the bleachers, her worried eyes darting to Eli's face. "Eshu is right."

We moved closer to our parents and found seats. I took in the celestials again, studying each of their faces and body language. Shangó kept staring daggers at Nana, but she ignored him. Ogun and Oshun glared at each other, their eyes brimming with anger. Even though the two weren't speaking, I had a feeling they were arguing with each other inside their minds. Eshu was the only one who looked more tired than angry. He massaged his temples.

I'd settled down to listen to what the council had to say when little stars flooded my vision. The chamber seemed to tilt without warning. For a brief, terrifying moment, I thought I would slip off the bleachers and fall into space. It took me a few seconds to realize what was happening. I leaned against Mama and squeezed my eyes shut.

"A dizzy spell?" Mama asked, hugging an arm around me. Her sweet perfume stirred as she held me steady.

I nodded, sinking into a familiar place of warmth and security. But it didn't feel quite the same, not while knowing the fragile nature of the veil and the enemies beyond it.

"Godlings, by now, you know the truth about who we are," Nana said, addressing the crowd. Her voice had turned soft, and her eyes shone with sadness. "We hoped that you would live long, peaceful lives, never to know the suffering and wars of our past."

Nana's words jumbled in my head and echoed in my ears. I clenched my teeth, trying hard to concentrate. Mama squeezed me closer to her side, and I let the dizziness run its course. Nana recapped the events over the summer and told the new godlings about the Lord of Shadows and the Dark.

"What does any of this have to do with Winston?" his

mom asked, interrupting Nana. "Or any of these children? The veil and this Lord of Shadows are your problem." Several people mumbled in agreement.

"Destinee, the Lord of Shadows is everyone's problem," Eshu said, his voice gentle. "It will take all our efforts to defeat him again."

"Wait a minute," Destinee snapped. "You think that our children will help you fight this war? Have you lost your minds?"

"No one is asking the children to fight yet." Ogun held up his hands in the placating way that adults sometimes did to get little kids to calm down. "We only ask that they start to train in case it comes to that."

"I'm done with this conversation," Destinee said as the fog finally cleared from my head and I opened my eyes again. She had gotten to her feet. "Winston isn't training for nothing to do with this mess. We're leaving."

"So typical of you to be selfish and think about yourself first," someone said from the top row. "You don't get it. If the veil falls, the Lord of Shadows will come after all our children."

"Who do you think you're talking to, Cheryl?" Destinee whipped around to face the woman who had spoken. "Winston, hold my purse."

"Enough!" Nana said, her voice shaking the chamber. "Those who feel the same as Destinee can leave now. We do not have the time or patience to convince you of the danger. You'll see for yourself soon enough."

When Winston got up to leave with his mom, he glanced back at his friends, who still sat on the bleachers. He looked like he wanted to ask them to come with him, but he said nothing as he and his mom stormed toward the exit. Several other families followed them.

"You will do well to remember and keep your oath to this council," said Oshun, her voice too sweet to be genuine. "Whether or not you choose to help fight this war, you are bound not to reveal your magic to the human world."

Okay, this council meeting had gone all wrong. Half of the godlings had walked out with their parents. No one could blame them for being scared. This was a lot to learn in one day—I remembered how hard it had been on me. But we needed all the help we could get to keep the Lord of Shadows out of our world.

"For those of you left, I'll be leading daily after-school training to help you master your new powers," Ogun said. "It's better to be prepared than pretend the threat doesn't exist."

"What about Papa's soul?" I asked, tapping my foot to calm my nerves.

"You're not going back into the Dark if that's what you're thinking," Mama said, crossing her arms. Her voice was shaking. "Even if it means . . ." She looked up at Papa, who stroked her cheek. "There has to be another way."

"The other celestials will be here soon, and then we'll go ourselves," Nana said. "We cannot make a move until we are at full strength."

"That's in like . . . three months," I argued. "A lot can happen in that time."

"Maya," Papa said, his face pinched. "A few months is nothing in the life of a celestial, as there are other gods of this world, so celestial would include them. I agree with the council that we will wait for the others to arrive."

"Well, I . . . I petition the council as the guardian of the veil in training to let me go back to the Dark and save your soul." I swallowed hard.

Ogun cast an apologetic look at my parents. "The child has petitioned the council on her own, and under our rules, we must hear her out."

Oshun smiled down at us, and I felt like a worm on a petri dish about to be dissected. "We cannot hear a petition from you unless you pledge your allegiance to the council."

There it was—just like Obatala warned me.

My heart was beating fast. "We won't pledge."

Nana waved her hand dismissively. "In that case, you cannot petition this council."

"Oh, come now, Nana," Shangó said. "There is no such rule that forbids those who have not pledged from bringing forth a petition."

"I agree," Ogun added his voice. "We must consider the young guardian's request."

"Fine," Nana said. "On the petition to allow Maya, Frankie, and Eli go into the Dark to rescue Elegguá's soul, how does this council vote?"

Oshun quirked a perfectly plucked eyebrow. "Against."

"Also against." Nana shook her head at Eli, her mouth set in a hard line.

"For," Ogun said in his fierce voice.

"Also for," chimed in Shangó.

That left Eshu. He looked to Papa, then to me. "This is a hard decision . . . but I can't with good conscience send children on a dangerous mission. I vote against."

Their votes echoed in my mind. I couldn't believe it. How could they stand by and do nothing again? They knew what was at stake. We had to get Papa's soul back, and we didn't have time to waste sitting here talking.

"Elegguá, if you die, will the veil disappear?" someone asked from the bleachers.

"He's not going to die!" I yelled, silencing the chatter. "I'm not going to let him."

"I thought that you'd say that," Nana said. "We'll be watching to make sure that you don't go against our wishes. Be sure of that."

That sounded like a threat to me.

ELEVEN

I GET AN UNWELCOME VISITOR

AFTER THE DISASTER in the gods' realm, I headed home with Mama and Papa. Mama only had time to change for work and grab her stethoscope before she left for the hospital. Papa and I had dinner in front of the TV, neither of us saying anything. The surround-sound speakers boomed against the living room walls and made me jumpy.

I pushed around peas on my plate that had long gone cold. I couldn't stop thinking about what Miss Ida said in the Time Out room.

"Papa." I looked up from my plate. "Are you afraid that I will make a mistake, too?"

"Of course not, Maya," he said. "I know it may seem that the council is harsh, especially Nana and Oshun, but they have the best intentions at heart. No one in their right mind is okay with sending children to face the Lord of Shadows."

I bit my lip, realizing that he thought I was talking about the orisha council. "No, I meant after what happened with Eleni. Miss Ida told me that she let the Lord of Shadows into our world."

Papa winced, like me mentioning Eleni gave him physical pain. He set his plate aside. He never talked about his other family. Once I died, would he avoid talking about me too? It hurt to think that he'd have another family after Mama and I were long gone. "You never talk about her or the others."

"Maya," he said, his voice cracking like eggshells. His shoulders hunched over as he inhaled a sharp breath. "Not one day goes by that I don't think about them. Sometimes the pain is bearable, and sometimes it's as sharp as a knife. No parent should ever have to lose their children."

Papa picked up the remote and turned off the TV. The steady ticking of the grandfather clock filled the room. *Tick, tock. Tick, tock.* It seemed to be counting down to some unknowable future. Could I save my father's soul? Could we stop the veil from failing? Could we prevent a war?

"Tell me about them, Papa," I said, imagining what it would be like to have siblings. I thought about Eli and Jayla, how he adored her and she adored him.

Papa smiled as I put my plate down and tucked my legs

underneath me. "I met Lutanga on the edge of an aziza set-tlement near a river. She was fetching water for her village, and I'd just finished fixing a tear in the veil."

"Tears happened even back then?" I asked. "A thousand years ago?"

"A few here and there." Papa shrugged. "Nothing like what we started to see after the second war." Papa continued his story. "I hadn't expected her to talk to me. The aziza are wary of outsiders, even us celestials, but Lutanga was curious. Fast-forward a few years, we got married against the wishes of her family. They said that I would cause her nothing but trouble . . ." Papa's voice trailed off, and he took a long time to work his way up to talking again.

"Kimala was our oldest," he said, skipping ahead. "She was the spitting image of her mother, with a singing voice that would put Mariah Carey to shame." Papa laughed at that, and I laughed too. It was good to see him smiling again. "Eleni was a year older than you and the only one of the three who inherited my connection with the veil. Genu was my little one. He was only four years old when it happened. I can still remember his infectious laughter."

"How did the Lord of Shadows trick Eleni?" A shiver climbed up my back as I thought about the first time the Lord of Shadows appeared to me on the crossroads. He'd sucked the color out of our neighborhood — turning every-thing ash gray. "Was it through the crossroads?"

"Yes," Papa said, his voice hoarse. "I learned much too late that he'd been pretending to be her friend, visiting her in what she thought were dreams." Papa blew out a shaky breath. "She was training to be a guardian of the veil, too. She was smart, Maya, like you, but he disguised himself. He pretended to be in trouble so she would help him."

"How could she believe that creep?" I asked, shaking my head. He didn't strike me as someone who could even pretend not to be shady.

"Maya, the Lord of Shadows is full of tricks," Papa said. "If he were so easy to stop, we wouldn't be in our current situation. He is much too powerful and clever. Never underestimate him."

"I won't, Papa," I promised, but I worried that I already had. The Lord of Shadows always seemed to be two steps ahead of us.

Later that night, when I was getting ready for bed, I thought about everything Papa told me. His eyes had lit up when he talked about Eleni, Kimala, and Genu, and I wished that I could've known them. I didn't blame Eleni for what happened with the Lord of Shadows. Imagine someone abusing their power and authority to do something so horrible. That was what the Lord of Shadows had done when he tricked her. I had to find a way to outsmart him.

It took me a long time to fall asleep, and when I finally did, I slipped into a dream. Frankie, Eli, and I were on our way to school. It was a sunny day, and the birds chirped in the trees. Some of the players from the Jaguars dribbled a soccer ball down the middle of the street.

"Think of all the benefits of cloning," Eli said, excited. "I could pull pranks at school and send my clone to detention in my place. They could take my semester exams and volunteer for bingo night sometimes."

"What if one of your clones decides that he wants to replace you?" Frankie asked. "No one would ever know the difference."

"It's a risk I'm willing to take to get out of chores," Eli said, shrugging.

We passed the abandoned house on Forty-Ninth Street. It sat far off the sidewalk behind a rusty fence and tall grass. The fence squeaked in the wind, and a sign against the door covered in vines read WELCOME. The word was hard to make out under the grime and chipped paint.

Frankie and Eli kept walking, but I stopped in front of the house, feeling a cold breeze biting my skin. A long creaking sound filled the air as the door slowly opened. It was completely pitch-black inside, like the bottom of a deep pool that never got any sunlight. The darkness poured out of the door, seeping across the porch. It inched along the ground, drawing closer to the sidewalk. As I watched it ooze toward us, I could sense that something had changed in the dream. The darkness stopped at the fence.

"I'm dreaming, not on the crossroads," I said, not entirely convinced. Was I dreaming?

"It's a door," Frankie said, beside me again, her voice monotone.

"We can see that, genius," Eli said on my other side.

"Maya," a voice hissed in the wind. It came from the house. I could feel the Lord of Shadows on the other side of the door, watching me from the endless darkness. It wasn't a dream version of him either. It was the real thing.

"You can't be in my dreams," I said, as the air around me warmed and my staff appeared out of thin air. I took one step forward, and the glow from the staff pushed back the darkness. It curled in on itself, retreating toward the house.

"Maya, don't," Eli said, grabbing my arm. "He wants to trick you into going back to the crossroads."

A knocking sound came from the old house, like wood splintering and falling in great heaps onto the floor.

"He's at the door," said Frankie, her voice a whisper. "Don't answer."

I was starting to think that my friends were parts of my subconscious mind here to help me connect the dots. Eli represented the practical side of my brain, straight to the point. Frankie was the metaphorical side, warning me through invoking imagery. That was the exact opposite of how Eli and Frankie were in real life, which was another clue that this was a dream. The house was a path to the crossroads, and the Lord of Shadows had tapped it.

"Don't be afraid, little one," came his withering voice. "I'll make your death quick if you free me."

I countered his grim offer with one of my own. "Send my father's soul back through one of the tears, and I'll spare your life."

"Are you sure?" The Lord of Shadows let out a laugh that cut right through me. "After tonight, he won't need his soul anymore."

My blood boiled with anger. I was sick of his threats. I banged the staff against the fence, which sent a stream of light that pushed the darkness back into the house. The door slammed shut. He was gone and the link that he'd connected to my dream, broken.

"Maya," Eli said, shaking my arm.

"What?" I snapped as I turned to him.

His eyes were wide as he stared at something behind me. "The veil."

I bolted up in bed, heart racing, my pajamas soaked in sweat. I fumbled to flip on the lamp on the table and knocked down my stack of comic books. *The veil.* I gasped as my senses kicked into action. My arms tingled as my magic picked up on the tear almost immediately. It was

massive—bigger than any of the tears before. It was a gaping hole between our world and the Dark.

"Papa!" I said to the empty room, but as soon as I called
his name, I knew that he was gone already. The Lord of
Shadows' last words taunted me: *After tonight, he won't need
his soul anymore.* Papa was in trouble.

TWELVE

OPERATION GO DARK

I HOPPED OUT OF BED and changed into jeans and a T-shirt in record time. I could still feel the gaping hole in the veil as I tied my sneakers. My hands trembled so badly that my laces ended up in two messy knots. This was our chance. I had to make sure Papa was okay first, and when the tear was almost closed, we could slip into the Dark. I sent my magic down the staff to make a three-way call to Eli and Frankie. It was quicker to reach my friends with magic than go downstairs to the phone.

"I knew something was going on," Eli answered before I could say anything. "Nana woke me up about an hour ago and asked me to watch Jayla until Auntie Bae got here. Then she did her celestial thing and poof . . . disappeared."

"Um, guys, look outside," Frankie said, coming on the line.

I jetted to the window and drew back the curtains. Flashes of white light streaked across the sky as black ink bled from the shadows. It crept across the streetlights, cars, trees, like a black blob, consuming everything. "It's a distraction." I hadn't forgotten what Papa said. *Never underestimate the Lord of Shadows.* "There's a bigger tear in the veil someplace far."

"Can you get us there?" Frankie asked as I drew a circle with the staff and the first spark of magic grew.

"Yeah," I said, a second before I stepped onto the walkway of spinning god symbols and landed in her room. "Are you ready?"

Frankie startled at the window and whirled around to face me. "That was quick."

She was already dressed and slipped into her sneakers. I opened another gateway to Eli's room, which was a complete mess. He had clothes everywhere.

"Auntie Bae's watching TV," he said, pressing a finger to his lips. "Let's go before she hears your roaring portal or you wake up Jayla."

"It's not a portal," I groaned. "A portal is like bending a sheet of paper in half to connect two points. I'm building a bridge that'll allow us to travel at the speed of light—that's a gateway."

"Ohhh-okay," Eli said, squinting at me like the difference didn't matter. He couldn't have been more wrong. I'd seen Papa make countless portals this summer, and they were much faster than building a gateway when traveling greater distances.

"Eli, I know you're not up there playing music, boy," his aunt called from downstairs. "Go . . . to . . . bed!"

He cringed, then yelled back, "Sorry, Auntie. I'll turn it off."

God symbols shimmered in golden light inside my head as I adjusted the gateway to seek out the tear in the veil. I was still so much slower than Papa at it. This new tear was far—much farther than the one in California. The farther apart two points, the harder to build a connection. That was why opening a gateway into the Dark took the most time and concentration. I shuffled the god symbols around to build a new walkway.

When I finished, the wind shifted from cool to warm. It smelled . . . *salty*. We ran through the gateway, our legs pumping hard. We were breathing fast, but not out of breath. Thousands of god symbols spun around us—stars, moons, animals, plants, geometric shapes, and symbols that defied logic.

"All those kickball games this summer paid off," Eli said, practically patting himself on the back for suggesting that we start playing. "This is like a walk in the park."

I was about to agree with him, but we took one step out of the other end of the gateway and dropped. "Oh, crap," I screamed, tumbling in a heap of orange and blue everything with no ground in sight. A flock of seagulls squawked as we busted up their formation. Wings slapped me across the face, and I spat out feathers. I'd opened the gateway over an ocean. Well, that explained the smell.

The staff ripped from my hand and sprouted wings. I almost got my hopes up, but then it flew away and left us in the dust. "Hey, come back!"

I reached for the god symbols again, snatching them out of thin air with my thoughts. They spun around us like disco lights, pulsing, and slowed down our fall.

"I've got this," Frankie hollered over the roaring wind. She stretched her arms toward the ocean and let out a blast of energy. Waves sprayed everywhere. In a split second, a crystal blossomed on the surface. We hit the barrier hard. It knocked the wind out of me, but it held.

Eli sat up, rubbing his head. "Is that what it's like to skydive without a parachute?"

I climbed to my feet with my attention to the sky. High above the ocean a few yards away, shadows poured out from tear in the veil. A white light teetered below the hole, in the shape of a man. Papa! He glowed bright, and his light stretched out far and wide, pushing back the shadows. Farther down, Ogun sat astride a mega-size General, who roared, all six of his eyes glowing. Shangó wielded his double axes, chopping up the writhing shadows that slipped past Papa.

"Is it me, or is the hole getting bigger?" Frankie said, pointing up.

It had grown in a matter of moments. More shadows crawled along the edges of the tear. Some shot out for Papa and pierced through his celestial form. He faltered, falling back. Shangó and Ogun surged forward, cutting and slicing their way to him.

"Papa, no," I screamed. He should've been safe at home, resting.

I reached for my staff until I remembered that it flew away. I balled my hands into fists. I had to help Papa. Magic flared inside me. It buzzed in my ears like it was itching to burst free. Something fluttered across my vision, and I gasped as a pair of wings with a harness flew right into my chest. I stumbled back as I caught hold of them. Up close, I saw the same god symbols from my staff. Among the symbols were a sun, a leopard with raised paws, and a river.

I am the guardian of the veil.

I fumbled with the straps that got tangled in my clumsy hands. "Help me."

"On it," Frankie said as she and Eli both sprang to action. They wrestled with the black wings that beat around frantically.

"Oh, fun," Eli exclaimed, rolling his eyes. "Now I have magical feathers in my mouth."

I slipped my arm into the side of the harness he'd wrangled into submission. "Sorry! I can't seem to get my magic under control."

"Incoming!" he shouted, pushing Frankie and me aside. Darkbringers filled the sky, but they weren't coming from the tear in the veil. They were coming from behind us. Too many to count.

"We'll hold them off," Frankie said, her magic dancing on her fingertips like sparks of lightning.

"I've got your back." Eli pivoted so that he was next to Frankie and raised his fists before he went full ghost mode. "Maya, go!"

Ogun and Shangó broke off from helping Papa to meet the enemy in battle. Lightning cut across the sky around Shangó as he swung his axes left and right. Ogun and General tore through the darkbringers. But whenever Shangó or Ogun hit one of them, the darkbringer disappeared. Poof.

I flexed the muscles in my shoulders and found that the wings responded. Soon I was fumbling through the air, climbing up, even if it was the rockiest flight in history.

I'd made it halfway to Papa when darkness exploded from the tear, and too many things happened at once. It bled across the sky, blocking out the sun completely. Papa looked like a lone beacon on a lighthouse, shining into a storm. I pumped my wings harder. Everything was pitch-black except where Papa's light pushed back a small pocket in the dark.

"I'm here, Papa!" I screamed as I flew toward him. Wading through the dark felt like I was neck-deep in icy mud.

"Am I glad to hear your voice, baby girl," Papa grumbled. He sounded like he was being crushed under the shadows. "Help me push them back . . . Use your inner light like you did with the Lord of Shadows."

Ice crystals crawled across my hands and up my arms, and they burned like nothing I'd ever felt before. When I reached Papa, he shifted his shape to his human form, but his light still poured out. His skin was ashy gray, and I looked down at myself, too. My hands and arms were the same. The Lord of Shadows was draining the brilliant colors from our world and . . . *us*.

I concentrated on the energy building inside me. The color came back into my skin, and the ice crystals melted. The heavy feeling of walking through mud went away. Patches of blue sky broke through the darkness.

"Give me your hand, baby girl," Papa said, grimacing. His locs blew behind him in the wind, and even they had turned gray. He looked so tired. "We'll give one big push together to close the tear."

I squared my shoulders as I took his ice-cold hand. This was my chance to prove that I could be a good guardian of the veil.

"On the count of three," Papa said. "One, two, three . . ."

I let go of the energy that had built inside me. Light poured out of my chest, my eyes, even my fingertips. Our combined magic hit the tear, striking against the darkness.

"It's working!" I cheered as the writhing shadows hissed and drew back. The hole started to shrink.

Sweat poured down my forehead and stung my eyes, but I didn't stop until the tear had completely closed. We'd done it—Papa and me. I squeezed his hand, but it'd gone slack. I turned to see his grim face. His eyes fluttered closed, and he fell from the sky.

"No," I whispered. All the strength fled from my body, and I collapsed. I was falling too, but someone grabbed me. By the fire threaded through the white magic; it was Eshu, the god of balance. "I have you, young guardian," he said, his voice gentle.

He set me down on the barrier—where the cranky twins, who'd appeared out of nowhere, had taken Papa. I stumbled to where he lay, unmoving. I dropped to his side. Tears blurred my vision. "Papa," I said, pressing my head to his chest. His heartbeat was faint.

I looked up, squinting against the sun at Eshu. "Can you help him?"

Eshu shook his head, his eyes sad. "He's in a deep sleep, Maya. He will not wake until he gets his soul back."

THIRTEEN

THE GREAT ESCAPE

W E'LL TAKE HIM HOME," Miss Lucille said, as she knelt on one side of Papa. Miss Ida sat on the other side. Blue ribbons of light wrapped him in a blanket and lifted him from the ground. I clung to him until Eshu pulled me away.

I swiped angrily at the tears stinging my eyes. I couldn't stand that Miss Lucille was so calm, like everything would blow over and be okay. Nothing was okay. Papa was in a coma. Eshu hadn't outright said it, but that was what he meant.

"Why can't we take him through a gateway?" I asked. "It'll be fast."

"Faster, yes," Eshu said, "but less safe."

"I can make a safe gateway!" I argued, annoyed that he didn't trust me to get Papa back.

"It's not your abilities that are of concern," Eshu explained. "Your father is very sick right now. We need to be extra careful with him."

I couldn't stop crying and shaking. Frankie and Eli stood close to me, looking miserable, too. The Johnston twins floated into the sky with Papa. The light from the setting sun shifted around them until they disappeared.

"Maya," Eshu said in his tempered voice. "I won't lie to you. Elegguá is very weak, but he's still fighting, or else he wouldn't be able to keep his human form."

I glared at him, anger burning through my chest. "This wouldn't have happened if you'd voted for us to go into the Dark. You're supposed to be his friend."

Eshu flinched like my words had been a punch to the gut. "I've known your father my entire life. We fought wars together, saw the rise and fall of civilizations." The fire in Eshu's eyes changed from bright red to a cool blue. "You and your mother are everything to him. You cannot know what it was like when he lost Lutanga and their children. He doesn't want to lose you, too."

I turned my back to Eshu before I said something that would get me in trouble. It was easy for the orisha council to make calls on our lives from their celestial thrones. Meanwhile, the whole world was falling apart.

"I agree with the young guardian," Ogun said.

"As do I," Shangó added.

Eshu glanced up at the god of war and the god of lightning. "Yet you are bound by the council rules the same as I."

Ogun and Shangó had a darkbringer chained between the two of them floating in the air. He was short—at least half the celestials' height—with pale blue skin and white wings that fanned out behind him. His long black hair fell in waves across his shoulders. He wrenched his arms, straining against the glowing celestial chains, but to no avail. I glanced around, confused. I had seen dozens of darkbringers. "Did the others get away?"

"There were never any others," Ogun said. "This one can create illusions."

The darkbringer laughed, and it sounded like glass shattering. "Enjoy the little time you have left."

"We know what happened eons ago," Eli yelled with his hands cupped around his mouth. "We're sorry that people died, but that wasn't our fault. Everything was fine until you started coming to our world looking for a fight."

"How arrogant of you to think that everything was fine," the darkbringer spat.

Ogun raised his hand, and a small white blob slapped the darkbringer across his mouth. "You'll have plenty of time to talk when we interrogate you later."

Shangó and Ogun hauled off their prisoner, leaving

Frankie, Eli, Eshu, and me standing in the middle of the ocean. A flock of seagulls flew overhead, and a whale breached the water. It was almost as if the animals knew the danger had passed for now.

"I thought powerful darkbringers couldn't get through the veil?" Frankie asked, crossing her arms.

Eshu didn't answer, which was an answer in itself. I turned my attention to the veil, letting my magic sense it. "He got through the tear because the veil had completely failed here." I glanced up at the sky. "There was no barrier at all for a little while."

"So, we're doomed?" Eli said, rocking on his heels.

"No, not yet." Eshu cleared his throat. "Our young guardian has strengthened the veil with her magic for now, but it won't last forever."

"We're not giving up," I said to Eli. "I'll protect the veil as long as Papa is sick." I wasn't completely honest in front of Eshu, but Eli nodded, and I knew he got what I was saying. Operation Go Dark was still a go.

I peeled off the wings, and they changed back into my staff. I lifted my hand to build another gateway, feeling my magic itching to do something. The sparks flickered in the air — this time easier. I didn't need the staff, although it was comforting to have it. I looked back at Eshu, but he had disappeared.

"I can't believe the orishas are still willing to sit on their hands with everything that's happened now," Eli said.

"Should we go to the Da—" Frankie started to ask.

"I know it's time to go to school," I said, making sure to sound extra annoyed. It wasn't safe to discuss our plans out in the open like this. "We don't have to talk about that right now, do we?"

Frankie winked at me. "Oh, well, everyone knows how much I love school."

Eli rolled his eyes. Even I had to admit that she was horrible at pretending. Once we stepped into the bridge of spinning god symbols, I closed the gateway behind us.

"We'll go during the field trip," I said now that I was sure no one could overhear our plan.

"I saw the permission slip; we're going to the Field Museum," Frankie said. "It'll be the perfect place to sneak off into the Dark."

"The cranky twins will be there for sure." Eli grimaced. "They're like a bad taste that you can't get out of your mouth."

Frankie wrinkled her nose and straightened her glasses. "Well, we'll just have to create a distraction."

***

When I got home, Mama was sitting in a chair beside the bed where Papa lay completely still. "Every time Eddy left to fix the veil, I got this queasy feeling in my stomach," she said, her voice choked with tears. "I tried not to think about it, but I always worried." She stared down at Papa. "I never could get over that he was responsible for something as vast as the veil with no one else to help him."

Papa was still in his human form, but his skin glowed with white light. His frame blurred around the edges like he was slowly fading away. "He has me to help now," I said, biting my lip.

Mama rubbed her forehead. "Maya."

Before she could finish, I said, "The veil won't last much longer. If I had to guess, maybe a week, possibly less."

"Maya." She repeated my name, this time anguish in her voice. "I can't lose you."

"If I don't go back, then the veil will fail, and everyone will lose everyone they ever loved," I reminded her.

"You're growing up too fast." Mama let out a frustrated breath. "I knew you wouldn't have a normal childhood, but I didn't expect anything like this."

"I like being a godling," I said. "I am going to be the guardian of the veil with Papa one day. You have to let me be who I'm meant to be."

Mama hunched forward, her shoulders trembling. "I'm not happy about it, but I won't stop you from going back into the Dark. I've thought about this long and hard . . . and you're right. I can't deny what you are, and I can't limit your potential." She swallowed hard. "Our world needs you, Maya, but I don't have to like it."

"Thank you, Mama," I said, giving her a long hug.

Operation Go Dark was back in business.

Mama let me miss a day from school, and the cranky twins "missed" school too. They came over to keep us company. They even brought food—mac and cheese, baked chicken, and potato salad—so Mama wouldn't have to cook.

The next morning, I met up with Eli and Frankie, and we boarded the buses to take our class to the Field Museum. The Johnston twins, pretending to be seventh graders again, sat right behind us.

"There's a big chunk of plastic poking me in my back," Miss Ida complained in a squeaky voice. "Someone ought to do something about these horrible seats."

"What was that, Miss Johnston?" Principal Ollie said, looking up from their iPad at the front of the bus.

"Nothing but the big pimple growing on the center of her forehead," Winston said from across the aisle. He, Tay, and Candace snickered.

"The joys of being twelve going on thirteen," Miss Lucille said, sounding less cranky than usual.

"Wait a minute," Frankie asked as she turned on her knees to face the twins. "You didn't only change your appearance on the outside?"

Miss Lucille shrugged. "The orisha council thought it would be more believable if we reversed our true age to twelve."

"So are you stuck this way forever?" Frankie asked.

Miss Lucille shook her head. "No, it's just that it's more than an illusion. We're actually twelve for now."

"Who would want to go back to being twelve?" Eli frowned. "No one listens to us."

"Precisely my point," added Miss Ida.

When we reached downtown, traffic was backed up bumper to bumper. Several yellow school buses had already parked on the street beside the Field Museum. It looked like Jackson Middle wasn't the only school on a trip. That was going to work in our favor.

"Stay together," Principal Ollie said, standing in front of the exit. Kids were anxious to get off and pushing each other to be first in line. "We're going to have a picnic on the grass for lunch."

"I'm allergic to boredom," Tay shouted.

Principal Ollie narrowed their eyes. "I have a list of allergies for our student body. I didn't see boredom listed by your name, but nice try, Mr. Curtis."

"So, what's the plan?" Eli whispered to me.

"I'm going to bring Sue back from the dead," I said, winking at him.

"Who's Sue?" Eli cocked his head to the side. "Also, if

anyone's bringing someone back from the dead, it should be me. I have a special connection to the paranormal. Obatala said so."

"Sue is a dinosaur," I said, shaking my head.

"You are so weird," Eli replied.

"Weird, but really clever," Frankie countered, giving Eli a smug smile. "You just wish you'd thought of it first."

"Well, if it doesn't work, you can always Frankicfy people with your general nerdiness," Eli suggested as we climbed from the bus.

Most of the tour would've been exciting if I hadn't had more important things on my mind. We walked through the exhibits with a guide explaining everything in meticulous detail. We saw fossils, meteorites, gems, and precious stones. Finally, we got to the dinosaurs, and Sue stood like a giant in the middle of it all.

Sweat trickled down my forehead as I glanced around the exhibit. People snapped pictures and crowded around the dinosaur. She was nothing but bones, of course, but that made my plan even better. What I was about to do was risky and likely would get me expelled from school, but I didn't see any other way.

"And here is our most popular exhibit," the guide was saying. "Sue is one of the largest tyrannosaurs ever found. She was named after the explorer Sue Hendrickson, who discovered her."

People clamored to get a good spot to take pictures with the dinosaur. I wasn't sure that I needed the coin in my pocket to amplify my magic, but I squeezed it anyway. Nothing happened. The coin felt slick against my sweaty palm. This had to work. Papa was running out of time.

After a while, one of Sue's massive leg bones moved. It was a small tremble at first. Besides Frankie, who gasped, and Eli, who looked stunned, no one else noticed. That was, until more bones rattled like Sue was waking from a deep sleep. The kids closest to the dinosaur stumbled back, pointing and shrieking. People thought they were joking until Sue shook her leg loose from the wire holding her together. Then she opened her mouth and let out a great roar.

FOURTEEN

WE NEED A NEW DISTRACTION

THE CABLES THAT HELD Sue the T-rex in place snapped one by one, sending metal cords flying across the exhibit. One cable crashed into a brachiosaurus. Its bones shattered and rained down on the crowd. Another cable headed straight for a group of people hiding behind a map of the museum. It shredded everything in its path.

Frankie threw up her hands and sent waves of energy that wrinkled space. Her blue sparks forced the cable to go wide, barely missing the group. It slammed into a wall before falling limp on the floor. More blue lights flashed, flitting back and forth like popping firecrackers. Those were for sure the cranky twins.

"Well, that didn't go as expected," Eli said, ducking a stray bone that flew over his head.

Principal Ollie snapped their fingers to get the dinosaur's attention. Sue tilted her head to the side and looked at them through empty eye sockets. "Time to go back to sleep," they said, raising a hand in the stop motion. A white light grew in the center of their palm, and I did a double take. I'd known that Principal Ollie was an orisha since earlier this summer, but I hadn't seen them use their powers.

Sue's tail went limp, and she staggered forward like a eighteen-thousand-pound zombie, which had to be the worst kind of zombie ever. Before Principal Ollie could put Sue to sleep, another dinosaur slammed into them. It knocked Principal Ollie clear across the room and straight through a window.

"Maya!" Frankie gasped. "You shouldn't have done that."

My hand shook as I clutched the coin in my pocket. I hadn't woken the second dinosaur, nor the third or fourth. "That's not me!" I said, turning the coin into a staff. "I don't know what's happening."

"Maybe another godling coming into their powers?" Eli suggested. "That or your magic is out of control yet again."

When we started toward the center of the chaos, Miss Lucille stepped in our path. "Stay here," she said, taking up a position in front of us. She raised her hand and deflected dozens of raining bones. "Ollie and my sister will handle this."

"Miss Lucille, I know this is bad timing, but I have to ask you something." Eli dodged another bone. "Why are some godlings' powers stronger than others'? Like, I can only do the invisible thing."

"What?" Miss Lucille asked, her attention split between us and the chaos. Dinosaurs whipped their tails around, breaking glass and smashing stone columns. "I wouldn't say some powers are stronger. Some are just more specialized or peculiar."

"Specialized, eh?" Eli said, his face lighting up.

Principal Ollie climbed back through the broken window, looking frazzled. Their light gray suit was wrinkled and torn, and they had a smear of dirt on one sleeve. As the celestial drew closer, their body shimmered with white light. That was when I saw the dinosaurs had purple and black ribbons woven between the bones. I couldn't breathe.

"What is it, Maya?" Frankie asked. "Another tear?"

I shook my head, unable to speak as the same ribbons wove through Sue's bones. I didn't feel a tear, but it was him. The Lord of Shadows had gotten through the veil. But why possess dinosaurs? I pointed at Suc as she stumbled and roared against Principal Ollie. "The Lord of Shadows is controlling Sue!"

Miss Lucille cursed under her breath. "It can't be."

"It is," I whispered.

"We need to get you out of here." Miss Lucille pushed us

into the mammoth exhibit, which we found full. A crowd that had fled from the chaos gathered here after the fighting started. The exhibit was a dead end. The only way out was back through the dinosaur exhibit. By the sounds of crashes and shattering in there, that wasn't an option.

I glanced at my feet. This was my fault. I woke Sue, and somehow the Lord of Shadows had taken advantage of the situation. He was here, but not really here. I couldn't explain how that was possible. It was like when he created a connection from the crossroads to my dreams.

"Shouldn't you be helping the others?" I said to Miss Lucille, but she ignored me as she stood guard.

Frankie grabbed my arm, her eyebrows pinched together in deep thought. "I've been thinking about what the kishi . . . Charlie . . . said on Azur. About calling him if I needed anything . . ."

I was only half listening to her. "Yeah."

"What if I called him now?" Frankie suggested, her voice dropping low. "He could help us slip away from Miss Lucille."

"Call him, then," Eli said. "I'm pretty sure he forgot to give you his number."

"I've been thinking about that too." Frankie opened her mouth to explain but stopped when both Eli and I shook our heads. "Give me your phone," she said to Eli, who shrugged and handed it over.

She stepped away so that Miss Lucille couldn't overhear her. We couldn't hear either. As far as I could tell, she lifted the phone to her ear without actually dialing a number.

"Is she talking to herself?" Eli quirked an eyebrow. "She's finally lost it."

"There you are!" Tay said, stepping in front of Eli and me. All I saw at first were his alternating red and black cornrows. He was a foot taller than both of us, and I raised my staff in self-defense. I was in no mood to take any mess from Tay or anyone else.

"Whoa, calm down." Tay threw up his hands, his palms facing out. "I just want to talk."

"Quit playing, Tay," Eli groaned. "This is not the time to be starting something."

"I ain't starting nothing," he said, rocking on his heels. "I need help."

"Help from us?" I asked. Where were Winston and Candace? They had to be in on whatever game he was playing.

"Yeah, you." Tay glanced away, looking embarrassed. "Listen, don't tell Winston I even talked to you. He'll disown me, but I have to ask."

I frowned, keeping one eye on him and one on my surroundings. "Ask what?"

"I need to know how to unlock my powers," Tay said, his voice desperate. "Winston keeps saying that he doesn't know how he did it, but I don't believe it. He just wants to be the center of attention."

I didn't think the day would ever come that Winston and I would be on the same side of anything. "He's telling the truth," I explained. "The first time we showed powers, it was really random. We didn't call it."

"Wait, but there has to be some way." Tay narrowed his eyes. "You're holding something back."

"Um, we have to go," Eli said as we sidestepped Tay. We really didn't have time for this conversation.

Less than a minute passed, and Frankie walked back over to join us and handed Eli his phone. "We should have a new distraction any minute now."

A light flashed in the corner of the room. When it faded, a person wearing a blue hoodie stood with their back to us. I only caught a quick glimpse of his face as the crowd swallowed him up. I was about to dismiss the man when a scream rang out in the exhibit. Then several screams, all coming from that direction. People rushed away from the man in the navy hoodie.

"For gods' sake." Miss Lucille whirled around to face the commotion. "Now what?"

"I'm going eat you all," came a loud growl. "One by one."

I got a glimpse of a tusk of brown hair, a snout, and very sharp teeth headed straight for us. It was Charlie. Frankie had actually called him. He did the big bad wolf thing, huffing and puffing, even though he was half hyena, not wolf. But it worked.

"Is that a kishi?" Eli latched on to Miss Lucille's arm like he was scared out of his mind. "Don't they eat people?"

"Calm down, boy," Miss Lucille said in her high-pitched little kid's voice. "Kishi don't usually eat humans, but I'll take care of this either way. They are not supposed to show their hyena face to mortals."

Miss Lucille stormed off after the kishi but stopped after only taking a step. She looked over her shoulder at us, frowning. "Stay put; I'll be right back."

"Where are we going to go?" Eli said, waving his arm. "We're trapped between raging dinosaurs and a hungry kishi."

As Miss Lucille stormed off, I gave Frankie a fist bump. "You're a genius."

"I'd like to think so," she replied, looking quite satisfied with herself.

I took another glance at the archway leading back into the dinosaur exhibit. The last dinosaur collapsed into bones. Wisps of purple and black ribbons floated up from the pile and disappeared. Principal Ollie stood with their hands on their hips, looking pretty ticked off. I was relieved that they'd stopped it—whatever had happened. I still needed to figure that out.

"Let's go," I said as we pushed our way through the crowd to find a spot to open the gateway. We ducked behind a mammoth where some people were hiding. Eli turned his head invisible, and they knocked each other over to get out of our way.

"That was mean," Frankie said.

"Says the girl who called a hungry kishi to scare a bunch of kids," Eli shot back.

"This godling is really mad," Charlie said, his human face popping around the mammoth. Miss Lucille streaked across the room in her blue light form and tackled him. They crashed into cardboard display sign that read DON'T FEED THE MAMMOTHS. "Whatever you're planning, you better do it now," he said as Miss Lucille's magic wrapped around his chest, pinning him to the floor.

"I wish I had more time to ask you about my mom," Frankie shouted to the kishi.

"Let's make a deal," he yelled back. "If you make it through this, give me another call."

"Deal!" Frankie agreed as Charlie wiggled free of Miss Lucille's gasp.

Near a wall at the back of the exhibit, I pulled the coin from my pocket. It transformed back into a staff as if it knew my plan, which it probably did. I drew a wide arc in front of the wall. My hands warmed as the magic pooled on my fingertips. But my focus kept slipping like a fog had settled in my head that made my thoughts fuzzy.

It wasn't like this before when I had concentrated on opening a gateway near Papa. Something pushed me away—well, not something.

It had to be the Lord of Shadows. My magic was bouncing off some sort of ward that worked against me. The sparks sputtered and flickered out.

"Anytime now would be good," Eli grumbled behind me.

"I'm trying," I said through gritted teeth. "I can't open a gateway near my father's soul. The Lord of Shadows is blocking me."

"Just open a gateway anywhere!" Eli said.

"I can't open it just anywhere," I yelled back. "That could be thousands of miles away or another continent or . . ."

I groaned. I was wasting time trying to explain something that didn't make sense. I couldn't open a gateway close to my father's soul, so I had to think of another place fast. My mind raced as sweat glided down my forehead. If we couldn't go to my father's soul, then we'd go to a place that could tell us where to find it. I changed my focus, and the sparks grew into a walkway of spinning god symbols.

"It's ready!" I said.

"Maya, don't," I heard Miss Lucille say as we plunged into darkness.

FIFTEEN

WE TAKE A MUD BATH

THE GATEWAY SPAT US OUT beside a swamp in the middle of the night. My head spun as I took one step and bumped into Eli, who crashed into Frankie. I lost my balance and fell face first in the mud. I groaned. It tasted like ten-day-old gym shorts — not that I was proud to know that. Eli hit the ground too. Frankie somehow managed to stay upright.

"Maya, this may be your worst landing yet," Eli said, spitting out mud.

"Ugh," I said, my head still spinning. I squinted at the gateway, which was already closing, and pressed my palm against the edge. The sparks shrank faster and disappeared.

"The mud is the least of our concerns." Frankie glanced

at a campsite, no more than a dozen feet away, and the dark-bringers heading for it. We weren't in their direct path, but too close for comfort.

The lights from the camp cast moving shadows on the field. I bit my lip, hoping they wouldn't see us. Two dogs with glowing red eyes led the group. They growled in our direction as they yanked against their leashes.

I cursed under my breath. I hadn't meant to put us so close to danger—another one of my mistakes. I dug out my staff from the mud, and the symbols glowed, although I could barely see them beneath the murk.

"Wait," Eli said. He stretched out his arms to touch both Frankie and me, then his magic, low and humming, spread across us. It brushed against my skin as light as a feather. Our bodies shimmered until we faded out of sight. Scratch that. We could see each other and see through each other. I would never get used to Eli's ability to turn us into ghosts at his command. It was the coolest trick ever.

The dogs pulled away from the darkbringers and ran straight for us. The last time we were in the Dark and Eli used his magic, the darkbringers had been able to track us by our scent. We didn't have a chance against these dogs, which more than likely had a heightened sense of smell to start. No different from the dogs in our world.

"Eli," I whispered, "they can smell us."

"Wait, I think I can mask our scents," he said, squeezing his eyes shut. Something shifted in his magic, and it tingled across my skin.

"I have an idea," Frankie said. Sparks danced on her fingertips, and her eyes started to glow. That was a new thing —and even though she had mud smudged on her glasses, she looked fierce. "Just in case."

Frankie's magic wove into a pulsing net with a ghostly glow. She'd somehow joined her force field with Eli's magic so that it could be invisible, too. With Papa sick, I hadn't thought a lot about how our magic had changed over the summer. My staff had turned into wings, and I flew. I wasn't lightning-fast like the cranky twins, but I was getting the hang of this godling thing.

"I didn't know you could do that," I said.

"Neither did we," Frankie confessed as she and Eli stared at each other in shock.

The dogs turned out to be *not* dogs. Instead of fur, green scales covered their bodies, and they had a row of sharp spikes across their backs. What was it with the Dark and its deadly animals? The last time we were here, we had to fight off large birds with needle-like spines on their underbellies. I was starting to think that everything we encountered in the Dark would either kill or eat us. Maybe both.

We held our breaths as the creatures trotted right by us, and two darkbringers ran behind them. I eased out a sigh of relief as the rest of the darkbringers continued toward the camp. There was a total of seven of them — six taller ones surrounding a smaller one in chains. Two of them pushed him forward, and he kept tripping over his feet. He had cuffs on his wrists and ankles.

Frankie grimaced at me, and I shook my head. I wondered what the darkbringer had done to be in chains. I remembered how Commander Nulan killed one of her soldiers for going against her orders. Another darkbringer said that she'd sawed off someone's horns for giving her stink eye. It seemed like it didn't take much for a darkbringer to find themselves in a lot of trouble. I didn't get why any of them would serve the Lord of Shadows if this was how he treated them.

"You know what we do to deserters?" snarled one of the darkbringers, shoving the prisoner in his back again. He tripped over his chains and hit the ground. They were in the light now, and I could see the prisoner's chest heaving up and down. His head hung between his shoulders, and his hair fell in clumps, covering his face. He was so small compared to the soldiers around him. "You're going to the stocks. It'll be hard labor for the rest of your life, boy."

He couldn't have been more than our age, twelve or thirteen at most. I already knew that the darkbringers had no problem with recruiting kids into their war. From the sound of it, this darkbringer had run away from the army.

A chill crawled up my arms. The darkbringers were our enemies, but I hated the way the soldiers were bullying the boy. It wasn't right to put anyone in chains like that or make them fight when they didn't want to.

Another darkbringer hauled the prisoner to his feet by the back of his neck like he was nothing but a rag doll. I bit the inside of my cheek so hard that I tasted blood. The Lord of Shadows' ribbons had picked up Papa like that and almost killed him. I couldn't forget the reason why we were here.

The boy spat on the ground, but he didn't say anything as the others pushed him toward the camp. It wasn't until they were almost there that the two darkbringers with their hounds came back. One of them halfway dragged both hounds toward camp. The second darkbringer slowed when he neared the swamp. He wore all black against his cobalt blue skin.

"Don't know what has them all worked up," the one with the hounds said as he wrestled to get them under control.

The second darkbringer turned in a slow circle and peered in our direction. My heart slammed against my chest. "Something doesn't feel right," he said under his breath.

"Stop wasting time," the darkbringer with the hounds said.

The second darkbringer lingered a little longer, then he backed away. It was a good five minutes before we had the nerve to climb out of the mud. It was too risky to conjure some water to wash up so we wiped our faces and hunkered down a little farther from camp.

"Tell me there's a reason we're this close to a camp full of darkbringers?" Eli asked, cleaning mud from his phone screen.

"Of course there's a reason," Frankie said, looking expectantly at me.

"I concentrated on opening a gateway close to my father's soul, but something pushed me away," I explained. "I think the Lord of Shadows must have my father's soul warded against magic. When that didn't work, I directed the gateway to open somewhere that could help us find it instead."

"Maybe you can try again now that we're in the Dark?" Frankie suggested.

I squeezed the staff. The symbols glowed, and the wood melted into a puddle in my hand. It reshaped itself into a silver compass. The top flipped open, showing two hands, one silver and one gold. "Take us to where the Lord of Shadows is keeping my father's soul?"

The two hands on the compass trembled like they wanted to move but couldn't. To prove my theory, I asked another question. "Can you take us to the city in the Dark that's in the same exact spot as our Chicago?" The compass glowed bright, and the hands turned due north.

"So Dark Chicago is north of here, but where are we exactly?" Eli asked.

"If the Dark parallels our world, then we should see some similarities to help us figure that out." Frankie glanced around, wrinkling her nose. "There." She pointed at a tree. "See that moss."

"Looks more like a nest of wriggling worms," Eli said, and I agreed.

"Moss usually grows in swamps and savannas where it's hot," Frankie explained. "I would guess we're far south of Dark Chicago. We could be anywhere from the Dark version of Texas to Mississippi, even in South America."

"I think that's beside the point, Frankie," I said, looking toward the darkbringer camp. She was missing the big picture. The staff had brought us here for a reason.

Eli brushed the mud off his shoulders like he was the coolest kid who ever fell face first in a swamp. "Time to go invisible again?"

I nodded as I stared at the darkbringer camp. "The key to finding my father is in there."

SIXTEEN

GET IN AND GET OUT

WITH ELI'S MAGIC making us invisible, we snuck into the camp once most of the lights had gone out. First, we circled the perimeter to see how many dark-bringers we'd be up against if things went south. Frankie counted twenty on guard duty. I spotted another seventy-five or so darkbringers inside the camp, but it was hard to keep track. They weren't exactly lining up to let me count them.

I wondered why the darkbringers were out here in the first place. They were alert, but they didn't seem particu-larly nervous about an attack. They had to be guarding the camp for a reason.

The hairs stood up on my forearms. There was some-thing wrong with this whole thing. The Lord of Shadows had known the last times we entered the Dark, so where were he and crony Commander Nulan now? I supposed he was too busy ripping tears into the veil and figuring out how to send his ribbons to the human world.

The camp quieted down once the darkbringers climbed into their tents for the night. "What's that?" I pointed to the lone flickering light at the center of the camp.

Frankie adjusted her glasses. "I don't know, but I can feel the energy coming from it."

"It must be important," I said. "Let's start there."

We walked in a straight line with me leading the way. Eli kept one hand on my shoulder, and Frankie trailed him with one hand on his shoulder. For Eli's magic to work, he needed to be in contact with the people and objects he wanted to make invisible.

We passed between two tents through a gap where there was no guard on patrol. Wisps of smoke floated up from the smoldering campfires. It was silent except for the occasional soft snores coming from some of the tents.

Thankfully none of us stepped on anything that cracked or broke underfoot. I'd never forgotten that a twig had gotten us caught last time we were in the Dark. Now that we were closer to the light, my heartbeat sped up. It was the darkbringer boy—the one we'd seen in chains earlier.

The boy sat in the middle of a cage with his eyes closed, but there was no way anyone could sleep in that position.

The contraption was cruel, and I wouldn't have wished that on my worst enemy. Well, when my worst enemies were Winston, Candace, and Tay, that would be true. Not so much for the Lord of Shadows and Commander Nulan.

"Maya, don't get too close," Frankie whispered. "He might be dangerous."

"He might help us," I said, keeping my voice steady.

"What makes you think that?" Eli asked. "He can't even help himself."

I spotted an abandoned blanket near one of the snuffed-out campfires and got an idea. "Wait here but stay hidden," I said. "I'm going to talk to him."

Neither of them protested as I pulled away from Eli, and his magic faded from my skin. I was solid again, whole and in the flesh. I darted across the space and grabbed the blanket, which I threw over my head and shoulders. I approached the darkbringer.

Magic burned through the air as electricity crackled between the bars in the cage. He sat with his knees tucked against his chest, his wings tight against his back, and his face buried in his elbow. He didn't look hurt, but I wouldn't have put it past these soldiers if they were anything like Commander Nulan.

I glanced around to make sure no one had headed in our direction and whispered, "I can get you out."

The boy didn't raise his head or open his eyes. He didn't

move an inch. I got a distinct feeling that he was ignoring me. "Hey, are you awake?" I asked.

The boy fanned his hand like he was shooing away an annoying bug.

I frowned, flabbergasted. Did he just wave me off? "Are you being rude on purpose?"

"Yes," the boy grumbled as he finally lifted his head. He had large dark eyes that sparkled in the half-light of the crackling electricity. "Who are you?"

I was taking a huge risk by doing this, but I figured that if I wanted the darkbringer to take me seriously, I had to show him. I pushed back the blanket to reveal my face. His eyes went wide. "You're a *godling?*" he asked as if the word tasted like dirt. "How did you get here?"

"That's not important," I said. "I could get you out for a price. You help me, and I'll help you. Deal?"

The boy rolled his eyes. He seemed to decide that I wasn't worth his time until he saw my staff. "Those are the celestials' symbols." He turned his head and spat against the cage. His saliva sizzled on the bars. "Leave before you get yourself killed. In case you don't know, the Lord of Shadows wants your kind dead."

"Okay, I'll leave." I crossed my arms. "I'll go find someone who's got some sense and wants their freedom."

"Look around, godling. I'm the only one in a cage here,"

he said, glaring at me. "Maybe I should call for my guards, and they'll let me go for turning you over to them."

"You go ahead and do that." I narrowed my eyes. "I'll tell them that I was helping you escape, then we'll both be in big trouble." I was trying and failing not to sound desperate. My staff brought me here for a reason, and I needed to find out why. "What's the punishment for being a deserter?" I asked, remembering what the soldiers had said to him earlier. "I doubt turning me in will be enough to get you out of trouble."

The darkbringer studied his fingernails like I was boring him to tears. "What do you want?"

My stomach twisted in knots as I worked up the nerve to ask. The boy could still call out for the guards, but it was a risk I had to take. "Where is the Lord of Shadows keeping Elegguá's soul?"

"You're his daughter, aren't you?" The boy smiled, and the look in his eyes cut right through me. He had something to bargain with now. "The one they say broke into the Dark and rescued him. The girl who got Commander Nulan demoted." His smile faded. "I thought you'd be—"

"Be what?" I asked through gritted teeth.

"I don't know, taller," the boy said, grimacing. "More imposing."

I sucked in a deep breath to keep my temper under

control. This boy was as infuriating as Winston, Tay, and Candace combined. But I didn't mind that part about Nulan getting demoted. Served her right for being so awful.

"You're a fool for coming back," he said, clucking his tongue like I was some little kid. "You were lucky to escape with your life the first time. I doubt you'll be so lucky again."

"I guess this fool is wasting her time." I backed away from him. "I'll find someone else to help while you rot in your cage."

"Wait," the darkbringer groaned. "I guess I have nothing else to lose." He moved his face closer to the bars, and the light reflected against his deep purple skin. He almost looked human, which caught me off-guard. "I overheard some of the soldiers saying that the Lord of Shadows is at the Crystal Palace. He has many fortresses, but the Crystal Palace is the most secure place in the Dark. It's almost impossible to reach it. I bet he'd have your father's soul locked away there."

"Why is it almost impossible to reach?" I asked, leaning closer to the bars.

"Watch out!" the boy said. "There's a reason no one can escape this cage. The bars kill on contact."

"How do I find this Crystal Palace?" I pressed.

"The location is warded against magic. There are only a few people with a map that can get you there, and you happened upon a camp with one of them." The boy eyed a tent with the lights still on, and I made a quick mental note of which one. "I'm sure you already knew that, or you wouldn't be here."

I narrowed my eyes, not knowing whether to trust him. I couldn't get my hopes up, but I didn't think we'd landed here for no reason. "Why did you desert?"

The darkbringer flinched and glanced away from me. He squeezed his knees tighter to his chest. "It doesn't matter why. I just did, okay? I never wanted to join Command and leave my family behind. It wasn't my choice."

"They made you join?" I asked. Things like this happened in the human world, too, and no one stopped it. The orishas left humans to evolve on their own while the Lord of Shadows had total control of this world. In both worlds, kids were fighting when they should've been home with their parents or in school. It wasn't right.

"Are you going to let me out or not?" the boy demanded.

"I'll let you out once we get the map," I said. "It's only fair."

He perked up. "*We?* Are there other godlings here with you?"

"That's none of your business." I winced, annoyed at myself for that slip. "I'll be back if I get the map and find it useful."

"No, you won't," he said. "I may not agree with everything the Lord of Shadows does, but I don't trust you.

Godlings and humans are nothing more than the celestials' little pets. You'd take over our world too if given a chance."

"That's not true." He was really starting to get on my last nerve. "You're the ones who came into our world first."

"The world was ours before your father created the veil that killed millions," he shot back.

"That was an accident," I said, choking on my words.

He dropped his head to his knees again. "Whatever you say, godling."

I stepped behind a tent so he couldn't see me. I felt a tap on my shoulder and Eli's magic again. My friends faded into ghostly form before my eyes.

Eli shook his head. "I don't trust him."

"I agree," Frankie said. "What if he's making up this whole map thing?"

I didn't know what to believe. The gateway opened close to the camp for a reason, and I wasn't going to leave until I found out why. "We stick to the plan, get in and get out, but we can't leave until we see if the map is real." I pointed to the largest tent in the camp. The darkbringer had looked dead at it when he mentioned the map. "I have an idea where it might be."

SEVENTEEN

IS ONE MAP WORTH THE TROUBLE?

I HAD SECOND THOUGHTS about listening to a darkbringer who had no reason to help me. But there was something here. I had to believe that the map was real, and it could lead me to Papa's soul. Otherwise, we would have no clue how to get there with the wards keeping our magic in check. I had to rely on my instincts now.

I swallowed my fear as we reached the largest tent in the camp. Still under Eli's magic, I glanced over my shoulder at the darkbringer boy again. He had buried his face against his knees. His bony elbows jutted out at his sides, and his shoulders slumped. I felt a little bad for not freeing him yet, but I couldn't risk him double-crossing us.

There was a light on inside the tent, but I couldn't see more than that. I pressed my ear against the flap and listened for sounds. I counted to ten in my head to be sure. Nothing. Not even soft snores. I reached for the flap, and Frankie whispered, "Careful."

I was careful or as careful as I could be, given that we were in the middle of a camp of darkbringers. I pulled back the flap only a little, and the cloth ruffled against my fingers. The gap was only a slit but enough to see inside.

There was a high table covered in papers with no chairs. A small wooden trunk with a pair of boots next to it. Oh, and the glowing orb floating in the center of the tent. It hummed like the white noise machine that Mama used to help her fall asleep. Apparently, the constant humming was supposed to drown out other sounds, but I found it distracting. Maybe in this case, though, it could come in handy to mask our footsteps.

It made me wonder if technology in the Dark evolved around magic. Did they need fossil fuel to create oil or gas, or nuclear power to produce electricity? It didn't seem fair that the darkbringers had so much magic while humans had none. How were we supposed to protect our world if the Dark attacked with only the orishas and godlings able to fight?

I spotted a darkbringer on a cot in a corner with his eyes closed and his mouth open. He snored, his chest rising and falling steadily. We couldn't hear him until we opened the flap, so I wondered if the tent was soundproof.

I crossed the point of no return with Eli and Frankie on my heels. We had a lot of ground to cover. I spotted another table with papers stacked as high as Ms. Vanderbilt's math quizzes. Ugh, this place was a mess. It would take forever to search.

Now it was time to get to work. Eli kept one hand on each of our shoulders as we shuffled through the papers on the table. To my surprise, we could read the notes — thanks again to the last time we were in the Dark. Most of it amounted to receipts, ledgers, lists of soldiers and recruits. My heart leaped in my chest when I found a map. I unfolded it, and the crinkled paper gave off a low groan in protest. There was a pulsing black ink blob on it.

When I lifted it to see better, the black spot on the map inched over too. It was like a GPS ping. The map itself wasn't very detailed, but it showed roads, towns and cities, landmarks, and rivers. Nothing pointed to a palace, but I stuffed it in my backpack just in case.

Eli released his magic, and we shimmered back into sight. He was sweating buckets, and he wiped his forehead with the back of his hand. His face was pale and tired. "Sorry," he whispered. "I was starting to feel dizzy."

I hadn't considered that constantly using our magic could drain our energy, but it made sense. I'd felt a little of that before when I was first learning how to open and close gateways.

"It's okay," I mouthed, hoping he would get my meaning. Invisible or not, we had to keep looking.

Frankie bent over a second map spread out on another table. She ran her finger across it, her eyes following along. She shook her head when she didn't see a palace, but I tapped my backpack to tell her to take it anyway. She nodded and added it to our growing collection.

If the Crystal Palace was such a secret, the darkbringer wouldn't leave a map of it out in the open. I bit my lip as I looked around and noticed the wooden chest again in a corner near the bunk. I was halfway across the tent when the darkbringer shifted on the cot and cracked open his eyes.

He frowned and bolted up, but I was quicker. Before he could call for help, I pointed the staff at him, sending out two blue shots of magic back to back. *Bloop.* The first one hit him across his eyes and spread out like sticky slime. *Bloop.* The second one wrapped around his mouth. I got the idea from Ogun when he'd done the same thing to shut up the darkbringer with the power to create illusions. The impact of my magic knocked him back to the cot.

Frankie raced over to the darkbringer. Her magic stretched into long electric strings as she wove a force field around him. "That should keep him for a little while."

All three of us were breathing hard, waiting for soldiers to burst into the tent, but no one came. My theory about the tent being soundproof must've been right. *Sweet.*

"I'll check the chest," I said, still keeping my voice quiet.

Eli wiped a string of sweat from his forehead. "I'm not feeling so hot," he moaned before he took one shaky step and collapsed to the floor.

"Eli!" Frankie exclaimed as she ran to his side. "You're burning up."

"I'm fine . . ." He squeezed his eyes shut. "I just need five minutes to rest."

I glanced at the chest again. As much as I needed the map, I couldn't risk my friend's life. We would find another way to the palace. First, we had to get Eli out of here. "We need to leave."

"Maya, watch out!" Frankie yelled as an electric shock hit me in the back. My whole body seized up, and the staff slipped from my hand. I hit the ground hard. The impact knocked the wind out of me, and my teeth tore into my cheek. I couldn't move as the metallic taste of blood filled my mouth.

The darkbringer towered over me. He scratched at the blob of magic still covering his eyes, but there was a crack in the one across his mouth.

Frankie hit him with a ball of raging energy, but instead of falling back, the darkbringer seemed to absorb her magic. He grew taller, and his head almost touched the top of the tent. His nails, which had been normal only moments ago, curved into sharp claws.

The darkbringer advanced on Frankie, and she stumbled back. I screamed inside my head and fought against the electricity winding through my body. My insides were on fire, and sweat stung my eyes. I had to do something — had to stop him — but I couldn't.

The darkbringer flicked his fingers in Frankie's direction, and his magic hit her hard. She crashed into the table, which broke on impact. I blinked back tears as my friend slumped to the ground, unconscious. The darkbringer ripped the blob from his lips and turned to face me. "I don't need to see you," he said, his voice a low growl. "I can feel your energy."

Think, Maya. How could I stop him when my muscles still felt like jelly? I could wiggle my fingers and toes now, but that wasn't enough. At least that meant his magic was fading. I regained control over myself little by little. I couldn't let my friends end up like the boy in the cage, or worse.

"The Resistance made a big mistake attacking my camp." The darkbringer laughed as he began to claw at the blob of magic across his eyes again. "I suppose you're here to rescue the deserter Zeran, but you'll be punished along with him."

Wait. Hold on. The darkbringer hadn't gotten a good look at us before I sent the blob for his face. He thought we were from the *Resistance?* I guessed Zeran was the kid locked up outside. "Where's the map to the Crystal Palace?" I demanded, letting him think we were with the Resistance.

"Ah, you people are so predictable," the darkbringer spat. "You cannot stop what is to come—it is inevitable."

Okay, so not everyone in the Dark was happy with the Lord of Shadows, which figured. He was willing to start a war. A lot of people had to be against that.

"Was that your best shot?" Frankie grumbled. The darkbringer spun around as she struggled to her feet, almost falling a couple of times.

"Oh, this is precious," the darkbringer said, his attention back in Frankie's direction. "I do admire your bravery . . . The three of you coming in here thinking you could steal the map to the Crystal Palace and save your friend. You'll suffer a horrible fate for your treachery."

Eli stirred beside me—cracked his eyes open and winked. A second later, he went ghost mode and I could hear him moving in the tent. I gritted my teeth and rolled on my side, my hand finally closing around the staff. I hit the darkbringer in the back of his knee. He yelped as his legs buckled and he dropped to the ground. Eli turned visible again. This time he was holding the chest. He swung it wide and knocked the darkbringer out cold. Everything in the chest spilled to the floor.

"Now, that's a good shot," Frankie said, still wobbly.

I crawled over to search through the papers, looking for

any maps we could find. We would sort them all out later, once we were away from the camp. We'd been here too long already, and the longer we stayed, the greater the risk of getting caught again. My eyes locked on a black tube, the sort of place you'd keep a rare map. I grabbed it, my fingers slicked with sweat, and pulled out the paper.

The map was tan with black edges, but my attention went straight to the palace at the center. It glowed on the page, while everything else looked dull. From what I could tell, it sat at the bottom of where Florida would be in our world. I wasn't sure that this was the right palace since the darkbringer boy said that the Lord of Shadows had many. But it was the best lead we had so far.

"This might be it." I put the map back into the tube.

"Finally," Eli said, still looking pale and sweaty.

I eyed the darkbringer unconscious on the floor as I stuffed the map in my backpack. "I'll catch up with you on the edge of camp."

"Where are you going?" Frankie asked as she leaned against Eli.

"To free that boy who told us about the map," I explained my plan. "I promised if he helped us that I would, and I always keep my promises."

"Forget about him, Maya," Eli said. "Do you think he'd keep his promise if the situation were reversed?"

"Well, the situation isn't reversed," I argued.

I pulled back the tent flap and looked around. It was still quiet outside, with no other darkbringers in sight. Thank the celestials that no one had heard the commotion in the tent. Before losing my nerve, I jetted across the grass to the darkbringer in the cage.

"You came back," he said, stumbling over his words like it was such a big shock. I resisted the urge to roll my eyes.

"I told you I would," I said, pointing the staff at the cage. My magic shot down my arm, and the electricity crackling in the metal bars fizzed out. The staff had absorbed it, and I could feel the electricity buzzing against my hand before it faded too.

The darkbringer reached forward, his eyes narrowed. When his fingers touched the bars, the whole cage turned into silvery dust. Some of it fell into his black hair and shimmered on his face.

"Did you kill Commander Rovey?" he asked as he climbed to his feet.

I shook my head, surprised by his question.

"That was a mistake," the boy said.

I backed away from him, and when he said nothing else, I turned and ran from camp to find my friends. He didn't have to tell me that I'd messed up. I already knew that.

EIGHTEEN

WE GET A MAKEOVER

I WAS DUCKING in and out of shadows when a blast knocked me off my feet. I hit the ground and rolled, my body slamming into rocks and grass that poked like needles. I held on to the staff and whirled around to fight off my attacker. But there was no one. The blast had come from the darkbringer camp, where half the tents were on fire. I stared at the rising flames in shock. Darkbringers were shouting commands to each other and running across the field. None of them saw me lying there in the shadows, too shaken to move.

"Maya," Eli called. "We're over here."

I climbed to my feet and ran. My friends had crouched behind a tree that was as black as the night itself. White particles floated in the air around its branches like glow-in-the-dark gnats.

I leaned on the staff to catch my breath. "Are you both okay?"

"I could do without the lump on my head, but otherwise, yes," Frankie answered, standing up to her full height.

"What happened back there?" Eli asked, his eyes wide. "Did you set the camp on fire?"

"Of course not!" I said, offended. "I freed the darkbringer, then I left." I wondered if the boy had set the fire.

We couldn't stay here with the camp burning and darkbringers everywhere. I gathered the three maps that we'd taken from the commander's tent. I was going to call up some light so I could see better, but the map with the palace started to glow.

"That isn't weird at all," Eli said, looking over my shoulder. "A secret castle with a neon sign that basically says, *Come die here.*"

It was *too* convenient, especially since the darkbringer boy had said that the palace was hard to find. I pointed to the cluster of buildings sitting smack in the middle of our path. "It's our only good lead, but first, we have to get through this city."

Frankie came over to look at the map, her flashlight bouncing through the tall grass around the swamp. "Is there a way to go around it?"

I traced the edge of the city, which took up most of the

page. According to the label on the map, Zdorra was the name of the city. "Not without losing a lot of time," I said. "The city is massive."

Frankie pointed at a string of islands that curved below the Crystal Palace. "That's the Florida Keys in our world. That patch of dark spots to the west of us must be the Everglades."

"So, you're telling me that the Crystal Palace is a retirement home?" Eli laughed.

I frowned, looking up from the map. "What makes you think that?"

"It's in Florida!" Eli said, like he was stating the obvious. "People go to Florida to retire."

"People go to Florida on vacation, too," Frankie countered.

"It doesn't matter," I said. "We need to head south."

We trekked around patches of mud, alert to every growl and rustle in the shadows. Pesky weeds kept crawling up our pant legs until Frankie and Eli found sticks to beat them back. The weeds hissed and jerked out of reach, eventually giving up. Soon we reached solid, dry ground.

Flames still glowed in the distance, lighting up the whole area. Had the darkbringer I freed set the fire out of revenge? I couldn't forget how he said that I should've killed Commander Rovey. I had a real knack for making enemies.

Winston and his cronies. Commander Nulan. Now a new darkbringer who had the power to electrocute by touch. I guessed he'd have to get in line — right behind the Lord of Shadows.

I stared at the map again, noting the lines along the top edge that looked like markers to show distance. As we walked, the inkblot on the map moved forward so that it was under another marker. We'd taken about thirty minutes to get from one marker to the next. With four and a half markers left, that was another 135 minutes to get to the city. I ran the calculations in my head. "We should be there in about two hours and fifteen minutes."

"That's reassuring, but my legs are about to snap from exhaustion," Eli groaned.

"Stop being so melodramatic," Frankie said, but she wasn't looking much better.

I felt guilty about their conditions. "We should take a break."

Frankie cast Eli a sideways glance. "I don't need to rest unless he does."

"Nope, I'm good," he shot back, voice defiant. "I could walk for days."

Frankie narrowed her eyes and smirked. "We'll see who cracks first."

He gave her a smug smile in return. "I guess we will."

Eli and Frankie have always had the rivalry thing, but sometimes they were outright silly. Like now. Who made a competition about being tired? Sometimes it seemed like they had a secret code between them that even they didn't know existed. I felt a little weird about it, but I tried not to let it bother me too much.

We took turns navigating with the map. While Frankie led the way for a while, I brought up the rear with the staff in compass form, softly glowing around us. We were far enough from the camp that the smoke was in the distance. A twig snapped somewhere behind me, and I spun around.

"What is it?" Eli asked, rushing to my side.

"Whoa, where did those trees come from?" I said, scanning the edge of the forest behind us that hadn't been there only a moment ago. The moon was almost black, and the glow from it was a shade lighter than the night. Leaves stirred in the breeze and cast shadows that flickered in and out of my line of sight. "They weren't there before."

The compass transformed back into a staff in my hand. My feet were already wide in a defensive posture. I was ready for anything and everything. Giant birds with razor-sharp spines, flying serpents, vampire bats. Anything else the Dark wanted to throw our way. I might've been scared, but I wasn't backing down.

Frankie squinted at the woods. "I'm pretty sure we walked by several trees."

"Several trees, yes, but not a forest," I said as another twig cracked.

Eli turned on his best TV announcer impersonation. "Our young ghost hunters discover a malicious spirit stalking them in the Dark. Will they survive the phantom and his insatiable craving for human hearts? Find out next week on 'Adventures in the Dark: A Story of Mayhem.'"

"Not a good time for jokes," Frankie groaned. "You're the worst."

Every muscle in my body ached from the electric shock the darkbringer had sent through me. I stared at the trees until my eyes burned, imagining hundreds of eyes peering back at me. We waited for a few minutes, but we didn't hear any other noises. Commander Rovey wouldn't lurk in the woods, not when we had the top-secret map to the Crystal Palace. He'd do everything to recover it before we got anywhere near my father's soul. Reluctantly, I turned away, and we continued walking.

"Some things aren't adding up." I paused, running it all through my mind again. I thought about the darkbringer who attacked us over the ocean. *How arrogant of you to think that everything was fine,* he'd said. "If the Lord of Shadows is causing the tears in the veil, why hasn't he mounted a full attack? Why are the tears so random?"

"And why not destroy the veil outright?" Eli added to the list of questions.

"I don't think he can yet." I frowned. "Papa said there have always been tears in the veil, but they got worse after the second war."

"What changed after the second war?" Frankie asked as we saw the first houses on the edge of the city.

I stopped in the tall grass. I couldn't help but think that we were missing something important. The orishas said that the Lord of Shadows had absorbed other celestials. "I bet he has a secret weapon — something that he's kept hidden like my father's soul."

Before we reached the city, Eli turned himself invisible to scout ahead. Frankie and I waited in the shadows by a tree oozing golden sap that smelled like honey.

"So, this might be a good time to don our disguises." Frankie slipped off her backpack and rambled through the contents. She pulled out her stash of face paint and costume props.

Frankie had gotten the idea to pick up supplies from the pop-up Halloween store on Ashland Avenue. We might not have been able to fool anyone up close, but at least we shouldn't stand out as much. It made me realize how much I missed some of my old life — dressing up for Halloween, riding my bike, hanging out at the park. I hadn't even had time to keep up with reading the latest Oya comics. It would be nice to have a day when I didn't have to worry about the world coming to an end.

"This is smudge-free and should last up to twelve hours," Frankie said, opening up the first tube. "The horns are the tricky part."

She put on her makeup first—and the final results could've fooled me. She had indigo skin with two curved horns, one on each side of her forehead. She'd sprayed the edges of her hair silver like one of the darkbringers we'd seen at Comic-Con. Being a genius and all, Frankie had a photographic memory.

"Now, your turn," Frankie said, squeezing out a different shade of face paint. This was cobalt to her indigo. She dipped a brush into the paint and swiped it across my cheek. It tickled, and I pushed down a giggle. It almost felt like we were back home and everything was normal again. "You look pretty good blue."

"I like your horns," I said.

Frankie made quick work of painting my face and styling my hair to cover the band that held my spiraling horns in place. They were black and looked like real bone, even though they were made of blocks of wood. "Are you okay?" she asked, her voice timid. "A lot has happened in these last couple of days. I wouldn't blame you for being overwhelmed. I sure am."

I shrugged. It was hard to explain how I was feeling. I

worried about Mama at home alone with Papa, and we were running out of time to retrieve his soul. "I'm okay, I guess." I remembered what the kishi had said about Frankie's first mom. "What about you with *everything* and the stuff with Charlie?"

Frankie glanced down at the palette of blue paint. She swiped the sponge back and forth across it like she didn't know what to do with her hands. "I guess I'm okay, too. I always thought that something happened to my first mom, but now Charlie's confirmed it. I hung around after our last encounter with the orisha council to ask if they knew anything. They said the Azurian celestials had investigated her death and ruled it an accident. I don't buy that for one second. When this is over, I'm going to find out the truth for myself. I owe it to her."

"I can help you," I offered. Frankie didn't say anything, so I reached out and touched her hand. I didn't really know what it was like for her to lose her mom, but I knew how scared I was for Papa. How afraid I'd been when he went missing and how determined I was to get his soul back now. I gave her hand a squeeze. "You've always had my back, let me do the same for you."

"Thanks." Frankie finally glanced up from the makeup, her eyes shiny. "I'm going to need it."

We both startled at the sound of grass crunching

underfoot. Eli shimmered from invisible to semitransparent to solid in the blink of an eye. He had a bundle of clothes in his arms and almost dropped them when he saw Frankie and me. "I got something to help us fit in," Eli said, "but I see I'm late to *that* party, gentle blue maidens."

Frankie wriggled her eyebrows at him. "You're next."

Eli looked like he was deciding between staying and running away. Frankie descended on him with a quickness. When she was done, she'd painted him slate blue. She didn't give him horns, although he did have a convincing barbed tail.

"How did you get these clothes?" I asked, as Eli tossed me a bundle, then one to Frankie.

"Hanging outside on a clothesline like in the olden days," Eli said, turning his back to let us change. "I figured we needed some new threads to blend in with the locals."

Frankie pulled on a bright green tunic with a slit where a tail might be. My matching tunic came almost to my knees, and the pants were pretty much black skinny jeans. I tried out the staff and found that the clothes didn't restrict my movement.

Our backpacks might be a dead giveaway that we were outsiders, but it was too late to do anything about them. "Ready?" I asked, sucking in a deep breath.

"Um, I've got blue paint slathered all over me," Eli said

as we set off for the main road that led into the city. As we got closer, the sky started to lighten at the first sign of the sun rising in the west — the opposite of the human world. I had a gnawing feeling in my gut that we were walking into a trap.

NINETEEN

WHY IS CURFEW A THING?

WE ARRIVED at the darkbringer city during morning rush hour. No one gave us a second glance as they hurried about their business, which was good. I didn't want to know what the people here would do if they knew we were three godlings strolling down their streets.

We walked past houses hollowed out of trees with bark for walls and leaves that pulsed with light. There were apartment buildings painted bright pink to yellow to rainbow stripes. Some houses had silvery rooftops that drank up the bluish light from the sun. Some changed colors like mood rings. Others seemed to breathe and sigh like they were conversing with each other.

A darkbringer with a toddler in his arms opened the

front door to a house that hovered six feet above the ground. Steps appeared beneath his feet as he descended.

Some kids wearing the same uniforms as ours flew by overhead. "Imagine what it would be like if everyone could do that back home," Eli said.

"Don't even say it," I groaned. "Winston is already so insufferable. Now that he's a walking torch, we will never hear the end of it."

"Things are going to be really different at school," Frankie said. "With so many kids with powers."

"But they'll never forget that we are the real OGs," Eli proclaimed.

Frankie frowned. "Original *Gangsters?*"

"Original *Godlings,*" he corrected her.

With everyone in a hurry, we got a chance to see a side of the Dark that we never would have under normal circumstances. We already knew what went down when the darkbringers came to our world. But we'd only seen the lackeys sent by the Lord of Shadows to stir up trouble. These were normal people. "They're not that different from us," I said, voice low. "Living their lives and whatnot."

"We could learn from each other if there wasn't an impending war and all," Frankie added, shaking her head. "Imagine what technological advancements and achievements in science we could share."

When we got to a busier neighborhood, darkbringers crowded the streets and the skies. The air buzzed with wingbeats and chatter. They sat on terraces eating breakfast. They walked pet impundulu and bloodhounds, and a creature that looked like a hairless goat.

"Not sure we're going to stay unnoticed," Frankie said.

There were fewer kids on the streets. I guessed they'd headed to school by now. As much as I didn't want to stop, we couldn't risk being noticed. We had to find a place to hide, so we didn't stand out. I wouldn't admit this to my friends, but I could have used a little rest myself.

We could see a massive park not too far from our location. It looked more like a jungle in the middle of the city, with overgrown weeds and unkempt trees. I figured the darkbringers' idea of a park was to leave the land in its natural state. We tucked ourselves beside some bushes far from the walking trails. Aside from the roots that groaned in protest when we first curled up on our sleeping bags, it wasn't a bad setup.

As soon as I shut my eyes, I was out and didn't open them again until it was pitch-black outside.

We raided our snacks and then Eli went to check the scene on the street. He reported the all clear, and we got started walking again. "According to the markers on the map, we should be able to get through the city in three hours," I said as we joined the crowds.

Someone looked at a screen that was counting down. "Thirty minutes . . . still time," they said.

Every screen we passed had the same timer, and I got a bad feeling about it. People hurried on the street, glancing at the clocks on the tall buildings every so often.

"Why does everyone look so nervous?" Frankie asked as we walked with our heads down.

"I don't know, but I don't like it," Eli answered her.

As we continued south through the city, the map blurred as the ink moved around. Before, it had been only a faded rough draft of buildings, waterways, and roads. Now the city covered most of it, and the Crystal Palace was a speck in the distance. "The map changed," I said, accidentally catching a darkbringer's attention.

"What are you children still doing out this late?" the woman asked, stepping into our path. She hugged two bags of groceries to her chest. Her dark eyes lingered on our uniforms. "Why are you all wearing that ridiculous makeup at your age?"

"We had extra work at school," Frankie volunteered an excuse. "And the makeup was for a class experiment on skin pigmentation."

"Curfew's in fifteen minutes," the woman said, heading for the building next to us. "You best get inside before the city patrol sees you."

"Wait, we're from the south side, and we don't have

anyone to pick us up," I called after her. "Any idea how we can get home faster?"

"Take the rail like everyone else," the woman replied impatiently.

"Where is the rail, and do we need money?" Frankie asked.

The woman squinted. "What is money?"

Oh, that didn't translate well, or at all.

"Credits?" Frankie tried again.

"The rail is two blocks that way," the woman said, not seeming to understand that word either. "You'll see the signs. I hope you'll get let off with a warning for breaking curfew. Good luck."

We hurried in the direction the woman had pointed out. A sign read RAPID RAIL SYSTEM, which reminded me of the Chicago Transit Authority back home. Before we could go down the steps, a horn blew across the city, and we froze in place. Projections flickered to life across every face of the buildings. I couldn't believe what I was seeing—*who* I was seeing. I clutched the map hard in my fist.

"Holy crap," Eli mumbled under his breath. "Is that . . ."

"Do you want the truth or a lie?" Frankie retorted, still staring up at one of the projections. It was a recording, but it still shot a chill through my spine.

The screen read CHIEF OF ORDER.

I gritted my teeth, hardly able to believe my own eyes.

The aziza stared at us from every angle. She was every bit as beautiful and as terrifying as I remembered. Golden-brown skin, broad nose, raven-dark eyes, lips painted black. She wore a new shiny gray uniform with a silver badge pinned to her jacket. The last time we were in the Dark, she'd been in command of the soldiers on our trail.

"Citizens of Zdorra," Nulan said in her familiar slippery sweet voice. "It is my duty as chief of order to remind you that curfew is in five minutes. Anyone caught outside without proper authorization will be severely punished."

By the time she finished speaking, most of the street had cleared. Aside from us, there were only a few stragglers. At least they had somewhere to go. We didn't. My pulse throbbed against my eardrums as we jetted down the steps to the rail. We had to get through the city before Nulan found out we were ever here. We'd gotten her demoted from her position, and knowing her, she'd want revenge.

TWENTY

My second-worst nightmare

I F THE LORD OF SHADOWS was my worst nightmare, then
Commander Nulan, aka Chief of Order Nulan, was my
second worst. As we rushed down the steps to the train, we
saw holographic projections of her against the walls. She
had the same twisted smile that she'd worn when she tried
to kill my friends and me twice. The text below her photo
read *Tap here for a message from Zdorra's chief of order.*

"No, thank you," I said, as we jogged down too many
steps to count.

"How is this a demotion?" Eli asked, breathing hard.
"She's got a whole city to boss around now."

We landed in the busy station with harsh fluorescent
light that hurt my eyes. Darkbringers strolled back and forth
across the vast room that had so many signs that it made

my head spin. It was like no subway station I'd ever seen. No turnstiles to tap your Ventra card to pay. No musicians serenading the crowd with popular songs. No one talking or texting on their phones or listening to music either. I noticed something else too. They all wore silver triangular pins on their collars. I hadn't noticed that earlier. That had to be why everyone was staring at us. That and our awful makeup.

A woman passed by us with a little kid tugging at his pin before she hissed, "Stop that." The boy poked out his bottom lip, but he did as he was told.

"Are you thinking what I'm thinking?" Frankie asked, eyeing the pins, too.

"Hall passes," I said, dread filling my belly.

Here was my theory. Some people had special permission to be out after curfew. The triangle pins were a kind of badge, and we wouldn't get far without them.

"We need those badges." I glanced at where Eli had been moments ago. I felt terrible about stealing clothes and now the badges, but what other choice did we have? We couldn't afford to draw attention to ourselves.

"On it," came Eli's disembodied voice.

How had he transformed into ghost mode in the middle of a crowd without anyone noticing?

"Unauthorized use of magic detected," droned a pleasant

voice over a speaker. "Please await the arrival of the city patrol for immediate arrest."

Scratch that no-one-noticed part from the record.

"Ugh, forget about that announcement," I said, my heart racing. "We need to catch the train that'll get us closest to the palace."

"There's a map of the rail system over there." Frankie pointed to a wall. "We just need to find a landmark to follow."

I pulled out the darkbringer map. The palace was on the other side of a river and a scatter of houses on the southernmost edge of the city.

"What about this building?" I said, noticing the one labeled ANTIQUITIES. In social studies, we learned that antiquities meant really old. "I think it might be a museum, and it's on the south edge of the city."

Frankie looked down at the darkbringer map, then scanned the map on the wall. "There." She jabbed her finger against the rail line that passed close to the museum. "It's off the yellow line . . . Well, it's not called the yellow line, but the rail system is color-coded."

We were so busy reading the signs that we didn't see the two darkbringers until they were in our faces. From their dark uniforms and steel-blue prods, I guessed that they were a part of the city patrol.

One of them tapped a tablet that looked like an iPad. "They're clean," he said. "No residual magic detected. It wasn't them."

His partner, the taller of the two, stared down his nose at us. He looked like he was going to reach out and swipe some of the blue paint from my face and say, *Gotcha, little godlings*. "Where are your Exemption Passes?" he demanded.

"We have them here." Frankie whipped off her backpack and rifled through it. "I had it just a moment ago," she said, stalling until Eli got back. "It's here somewhere."

I followed her lead. "Maybe they're in my bag."

"Per section A56.1," recited the darkbringer with the tablet. "Citizens must wear their E-passes at all times after curfew. Citizens found in violation will be arrested onsite and taken to the stocks."

"The stocks?" I mumbled. "That's rather archaic."

The taller darkbringer gripped his prod like he was itching for a fight. "What did you say?"

"She said that's rather mosaic." Frankie pointed at the tiles on the floor. They were a uniform gray that reflected a prism of colors from the lights overhead.

We were starting to draw attention now. People stopped to stare and whispered to their companions. They stood around, waiting for what would happen next.

"Who would let their children outside without E-passes?" one man said. "What a shame."

"No one ever comes back from the stocks with their right minds," explained another. "Always missing a body part too."

An older woman shook her head. "That's if they come back at all."

"By the law of the chief of order, you are under arrest," the patrol officer with the tablet declared.

I felt a faint pressure against my side and said, "Wait! I have it." I snatched the E-pass from my pocket. Eli had come through again. "Here it is," I said, pinning the pass to my collar.

Both officers rolled their eyes as if disappointed that they couldn't haul me off to the stocks. Some of the bystanders sighed in relief. It seemed that they were not fans of the stocks either.

"And you," the taller darkbringer turned to Frankie, but she was in the middle of pinning an E-pass to her shirt, too. He raised his left arm, revealing a glass ring on the back of his hand. The ring flashed once when he reached in Frankie's direction. It did the same when he reached toward me.

Two miniature holographic photos of darkbringers materialized above the ring. They were facing the patrol, and I could only see the backs of their heads. One had a red 'fro like Ms. Vanderbilt, and the other one had antlers that curved down to the nape of her neck. Now we knew for sure that the badges were IDs — and those darkbringers looked nothing like us.

"Would you believe me if I said I got my horns altered?" I said, slipping my hand into my pocket to feel for the coin. I didn't want to cause a scene, but I wouldn't let these darkbringers arrest us either.

"I changed my hair color?" Frankie said, like she was asking them a question.

A crash from behind the patrol caught their attention. Someone screamed, and a lot of things happened at once. Several people pushed and shoved, and sparks flashed farther down the hall.

"Unauthorized use of magic detected," the voice droned again. "Please await the arrival of the city patrol for immediate arrest." The patrol pushed past us and rushed toward the disturbance.

I let out a shaky breath. "That was nerve-wracking."

"You're telling me," Eli whispered so close to my ear that I almost jumped out of my skin. He was still invisible and keeping his voice low.

"What took you so long?" Frankie slung her backpack across her shoulder again.

"You try unpinning a badge that's right under someone's nose without getting caught," Eli challenged. "Let's see how long it takes you."

"Never mind that," I said. "You have to stay invisible for now. This station has a way to detect when we use magic."

When we finally found the sign pointing to the right train, we had to get a lift to the level above us. By lift, I meant literally take an air pocket. We lined up along the wall and waited for the air to lift us to the next level. It hit us without warning, and the ride was a little bumpy. I clutched the headband that held my horns in place so that they wouldn't fall off.

The platform, at least, was less busy, with no patrol officers. We'd only been there a moment before we heard the gentle hum of the train. Soon green flames sparked to life over the single rail, and a glass tube pulled into the station. It hovered above the rail and the green flames that seemed to support its weight. The doors didn't slide open; they melted, and a few people exited the train at the station. The whole thing reminded me of a glass beaker set over flames.

"Here goes nothing," I said as we boarded with a small group.

We took three seats in a corner, hoping that no one would plop down in the middle seat on top of Eli. Frankie dug around in her backpack and removed a cloth to wipe the smudges from her glasses.

The train zipped through the tunnel alongside dark

walls that glowed as we passed. I thought that it had something to do with the green fuel that kept the train afloat and stable. We went through several stations with people getting on and off. Unlike the CTA, which always smelled a little funky, this train smelled sort of pleasant.

I was starting to relax when a group of soldiers stepped on the train. I made eye contact with the darkbringer from the camp, Commander Rovey, who flashed me a crooked smile that said *gotcha*. I pulled the coin from my pocket, ready to turn it back into a staff. But the darkbringer beside the commander raised his hand, and an invisible net pinned me to the seat. The coin dropped to the floor and rolled out of sight.

"Hey," a passenger yelled. "No magic on public transportation."

"Shut up," one of the soldiers said, waving his finger in the man's face. The man balled his hands into fists, but he didn't protest again.

"Unauthorized use of magic detected," announced a calm voice over the loudspeaker again. That voice was starting to get on my nerves. "Please await the arrival of the city patrol for immediate arrest."

"I don't think these guys care about the city patrol," Frankie said, struggling against the net.

I struggled too, but it was no use. The net had pinned

Frankie's hands and the backpack against her chest. My hands were jammed up against my sides.

"Little thieves and arsonists," said Commander Rovey. "You thought I would let the Resistance come into my camp and steal from me?"

"Wait . . . what?" I protested. "We didn't burn down your camp."

"Don't you want to know how I found you?" the commander asked, leaning close to my face. "My magic leaves a distinct mark that I can track for hours. Where is Zeran?" He had a cutting edge to his tone.

When he said his magic left a mark, I thought about the poodle who always peed on the Johnston twins' tulips. He was marking his territory. "Well, in that case, I'm glad your camp burned down," I shot back, which I knew wasn't a nice thing to say, but he was asking for it.

The doors opened at the next station, and a group of patrol officers stepped on the train. My heart dropped to my stomach. Nulan stood in front of the group. She was in a dark gray uniform like the other patrol officers, except hers was ten times nicer. She looked across to the commander with a smile deadly enough to crack ice.

Crap. We had enemies on both sides, and my staff was currently under a bench.

"Commander Rovey." She spat his name like it was

poison on her tongue. "So you're the one causing an uproar after curfew. Must I remind you of the basic rules of civil law? Nonessential magic is only permitted on private property within city limits, or have you forgotten?"

I had a lot to learn about the Dark world. What was nonessential versus essential magic?

"COO Nulan," the commander said, with no pretense of politeness. "Shouldn't you be at your big, comfortable desk, not out in the field? The life of a bureaucrat fits you."

"I would be out in the field if you hadn't stolen my job," Nulan said through gritted teeth.

Rovey smiled, his nostrils flaring. "And now I'll get another promotion for capturing these Resistance fighters."

Nulan's shoulders tensed as she followed Commander Rovey's gaze to me. Her brown eyes narrowed into catlike slits as she cursed. She took one step in our direction as a slim knife materialized in her hand out of thin air. She broke into a conniving smile that sent ice through my veins. "They aren't Resistance, you fool," she said. "They're godlings, and they're mine."

TWENTY-ONE

THE ENEMY OF MY ENEMY IS MY ENEMY

NULAN'S BLADE SCRAPED against the invisible net as she thrust the knife underneath my chin. The net shimmered with white light for a moment, revealing itself, but faded again. Her brown eyes sparkled with flecks of gold, and she pressed the knife a little closer. As soon as the cold metal bit into my throat, she stopped. I leaned back hard against the seat. Nulan was so close to me that I could feel her breath on my face and her magic tingling in the knife.

Her lips trembled as she said, "You cost me my job, *Maya*." She paused and pulled back the knife. "If our lord did not need you alive, I would gut you myself."

I remembered the last time I'd seen her, lying on the floor in the gym after Papa had turned her soldiers into dust. He hadn't wanted to hurt them, but she gave him no choice. I tried to think of something snappy to say, but I only felt scared as I stared at the aziza. She wanted me dead. That was a no-brainer. But why did the Lord of Shadows *need* me alive?

"He didn't say alive and well, though," Nulan added, her voice calm. "He couldn't fault me for taking out one of your pretty little eyes or cutting off your nose."

"Leave her alone," Frankie yelled.

"Where's your other little friend?" Nulan asked. "The one who can make himself invisible."

"He's not here," I lied, but Nulan flicked her wrist and drove the knife straight for the seat between Frankie and me.

"No," I screamed.

I squeezed my eyes shut as tears slid down my cheeks. I could hear the crunch of the knife against something hard. When I opened my eyes, I saw it lodged into the back of the seat, but there was no blood.

"Where is that little godling?" Nulan asked through gritted teeth.

I laughed, relieved that Eli was okay. "Wouldn't you like to know?"

"Step aside, COO Nulan," Commander Rovey said. "I caught these godlings, and I plan to deliver them to the Lord of Shadows personally and reap the reward of my loyalty."

Nulan whipped her head around, and one of her wings clipped my leg. "What did you say?" she asked, even though that was definitely a rhetorical question. She'd heard him. "Do you realize that you are in my jurisdiction . . . my city? This isn't like in the field, where there are no rules."

The other passengers ducked around Commander Rovey's and COO Nulan's opposing forces. They fled through the doors on either side of the car, opting to go to another part of the train instead. I didn't blame them for choosing to run before the real fighting started. I wished that we could duck right out with them, but Frankie and I couldn't free ourselves. The net bit into our skin, and no amount of struggling helped. And where was Eli? This was about to get ugly and fast. We'd seen both Nulan and Rovey in action. They were deadly.

"What of it?" Rovey glared at Nulan. He moved his legs wide, with his hands hanging limp. Typical attack position. It looked like a neutral stance on the surface, but Papa had done it many times during staff training. "This city is of little importance."

"Even still," Nulan warned, "you do not want to challenge me."

"I think we're too late for that," Rovey said.

The four soldiers at Rovey's back stepped closer. One had flames ignite on his fingertips. He must have been a distant cousin of Winston. Another had spikes that grew all over her body. A second girl's eyes began to glow. The last one — the boy who'd trapped us under the net — cracked his knuckles.

Nulan's knife faded, only to be replaced by steel-blue prods, one in each hand. A vein of electricity sparked along the length of the prods. The four patrol officers behind her followed her lead. On account of her being an awful person, I didn't have the heart to tell her that Rovey could absorb energy.

Besides, let them fight. That was the only way we'd have a chance to get out of this. We could escape while they were busy trying to kill each other.

Nulan struck first as the train rocketed down the track. She didn't head straight for Rovey. She pivoted and spun as the soldier with flames let loose a firestorm at her. Her wings that'd been green, blue, and gold a moment ago changed to a bright silver that almost looked like metal. The fire bounced harmlessly off them.

One of her patrol guards leaped to the glass ceiling and scuttled across it like a spider. I didn't know how he could do that with the prods still in his hands. Once he was in enemy territory, he dropped from the ceiling, barely missing the spikes that shot out at him. He was quick as he crouched and jabbed his prods into the flame boy and the girl with the spikes. The boy's flames went out like someone had doused him in water, and the girl's spikes retracted back into her body.

"The prods neutralize magic," I whispered under my breath. That wasn't like the prod the darkbringer used against me at Comic-Con this summer. Maybe they could be programmed to do different things. The patrol officer hit them with another jolt that knocked them out. But before he could attack again, Rovey sent an electric charge that cut him down too. He hit the floor.

Nulan: 2

Rovey: 1

"Are we sure Eli's not . . ." Frankie swallowed hard as she stared at the spot where Nulan's knife had pierced through the seat. "What if . . ."

"If I had died in ghost mode, then I wouldn't have to change much, would I?" came his voice. He sounded like he was across from us but up high. Was he on the bag rack above the seats? "Did you miss me?"

"Absolutely not!" Frankie blurted out, but I could tell that she was relieved to hear his voice, too. "Are you planning on helping us?"

"Waiting for the right moment," he grumbled.

"Now would be a good time," I said, but I could already feel pressure against the net.

Commander Rovey had two soldiers left to fight against

Nulan's three patrol officers. The girl with the glowing eyes stepped around her fallen comrades. One of the patrol officers swung his prod at her and froze midstrike. He didn't turn into stone like in the stories about Medusa, but he looked like a department store mannequin. The girl turned her gaze on the other two officers, but they closed their eyes. Smart.

The boy with the power to make invisible nets stiffened at the Medusa girl's side, his jaw clenched tight. He seemed to be struggling as he turned to her, his hands shaking. He gritted his teeth like he was fighting something inside himself. I looked to the officer with sweat beading on his forehead—he was mimicking the boy's moves. Wait, no. He was making the boy turn on the Medusa girl. The boy lifted his hands and flung out a net that slammed Medusa into the wall. The impact cracked the glass, and the train swayed hard to the left. I could hear people screaming on the next cars. The girl slid to the floor, unconscious.

Nulan: 3

Rovey: 2

The boy shook his head, seeming to come out of his trance altogether. He screamed as he raised his hands again. He hit the last two officers with a net that pinned them to the ground, just as the train finally righted itself. Sweat poured down his face as he dropped to his knees and passed out, too.

Nulan: 4

Rovey: 4

Eli finally cut through my net and thrust the coin into my hand. It was hot from being in his pocket, but I was relieved to have it again. With a deep moan, it transformed into staff form.

Nulan and Rovey moved toward each other — the final two standing. We needed to go now. Nulan's back was to us, but Rovey saw me stand up and sent a jolt of energy my way. I braced myself for the pain, but it never came. Electricity sparked in front of me, illuminating a shape that was unmistakably Eli. He fell to his knees and slumped to his side.

"No," I yelled, as Nulan struck Rovey with one of the prods.

I sent my magic down the staff cut the net from Frankie. Once she was free, she knelt beside Eli, who remained visible but was out cold.

"Antiquities is next," a voice announced. "Exit right and have a nice day."

"That's our stop," Frankie said, as we hoisted Eli up between us.

As we neared the station, two dozen patrol officers waited on the platform with their prods ready. Nulan would have backup soon. Rovey locked Nulan in a bear hug, and electricity shot through her. Her whole body shook, and the prods dropped from her hands. Rovey laughed as she went limp in his arms. I didn't feel sorry for her.

I tried to open a gateway so we could escape, but I must've been too distracted, because the sparks fizzled out. I tried a second time, and the same thing. This couldn't be happening right now.

Nulan head-butted Rovey. He dropped her, and she crashed to the ground. Rovey stumbled back, looking dazed and confused while Nulan gave him a vicious smile. "This is the end of the line for you," she said as knives appeared in her hands.

"Maya, let's go," Frankie said, her voice low.

I wouldn't dare turn my back on Nulan—she was too dangerous. Instead, I guarded our rear, and Frankie focused on what was ahead of us. Rovey sparked with a new surge of electricity. The fight wasn't over yet, not by a long shot. When we reached the door between the two cars, a seam split down the middle and the door melted open. We entered into new chaos. People were in full panic mode.

The train came to a stop, and everyone rushed out. As we did, the patrol officers shoved their way into the car with Nulan and Rovey. Sparks lit up the platform. Windows shattered. Metal twisted and bent. The wall near the track cracked and rained down sharp bits of stone. Now I understood why there were rules about not using magic in public. It was too dangerous, and people were unpredictable.

Frankie and I carried Eli between us, but we were moving too slow, and the crowd would be out of the station before us.

"Let me help you," said a tall woman who stepped in our path. "I'm a doctor."

I was suspicious, but we were losing ground. "Okay."

The woman pressed a finger to Eli's forehead, and his eyes popped wide open. He shook his head. "That was some train ride."

"Can you walk?" Frankie asked.

Eli nodded as he took a few shaky steps.

"Thank you," I said to the darkbringer, but she'd disappeared back into the crowd.

We followed the crowd toward the exit signs and took air pockets up to the ground level. Soon we were on the streets again in the dead of night. We found an alley to rest for a moment and catch our breath.

According to the map, we were almost out of the city. It would take another twenty minutes or so to be clear of it. We trekked through the streets again, keeping to the shadows.

I couldn't stop thinking about Nulan and Rovey. They had tried to kill each other just so one of them could have the honor of turning us over to the Lord of Shadows. I couldn't get Nulan's words out of my head either. The Lord of Shadows wanted me alive. No. Her exact words were that he *needed* me alive. I didn't like the sound of that. He was up to something. That was bad enough. But if he needed me to make his latest evil plans work, then I was in big trouble.

TWENTY-TWO

SOMETHING'S NOT RIGHT

FTER WE PASSED the city limits, we expected to see a
river and a scattering of houses, but we got a rude
awakening. We stood face-to-face with a mountain range.
I pulled out the map again, tracing our path, looking for
where we made a wrong turn. How could I mess this up?

Eli leaned on my staff while Frankie and I spread the
map on the ground. It showed the mountains behind the
antiquities building and its surrounding garden. "This
isn't right." I frowned. "I'm sure there was supposed to be
a river."

"I told you not to trust that thing, but neither of you
ever listen to me," said Eli under his breath.

I studied the mountains on the new path to the Crystal

Palace. "We should've known that if there were a map to the Lord of Shadows' hideout, it wouldn't be that easy. The darkbringer boy at the camp said that the palace was top secret, so maybe the map is boobytrapped."

"I think you can drop the 'maybe' part," Eli said.

I bit my tongue. This was not the time to be funny or cynical. Every moment we wasted in the Dark put Papa at greater risk. We had to figure this out, and soon. I glanced over my shoulder. The city loomed at our backs, watching our every move. Nulan was there. Rovey, too, if she hadn't put an end to him.

"Now that Nulan knows we're here, when she's done with Rovey, she'll come after us." I stuffed the map in my backpack. "We keep going, but we have to be more careful. I don't see another choice."

"Nulan said the Lord of Shadows *needs* you alive—so we can use that to our advantage, right?" Frankie asked, emphasis on the word *needs,* which only made my skin crawl. "She knows that she can't kill you, although she doesn't seem to have any qualms about killing us."

"I can see it now when she delivers Maya to the Lord of Shadows." Eli bowed his head and groveled. "She'll be like, 'O Lord, the mightiest of the mighty, king of slithery things, the god of the Dark, the . . .'"

"We get the point, Eli," I said, forcing down a smile.

Frankie fiddled with her crooked glasses. "Why do you have to be so extra?"

"The same reason why you have to be so nerdy," Eli retorted.

We reached a sign at the base of the mountain that pointed out several trails. "I don't know why the Lord of Shadows would need me alive."

"You're the only one who can stop the veil from failing with your father sick," Eli suggested. "He probably wants to guarantee that you'll be out of the way."

"I don't quite buy that." I frowned. "He could let Nulan or Rovey kill me."

"He'll have a better chance of winning if the veil is completely gone," Frankie said. "But I don't think it's that simple."

"Exactly my point," I mumbled to myself.

We studied the sign. Each trail had an estimated distance and time to get from one side of the mountain to the other. "The shortest trail is straight up," I said, "but it looks pretty steep. It could be dangerous, especially at night."

"Which is the safest route?" Eli asked, poking his head over my shoulder.

"The trail along the side of the mountain," Frankie answered. "But that one takes almost three times as long."

Even though I wanted to get to the palace fast, it didn't

make sense to take the most treacherous path. Besides, Nulan knew that we were desperate and might think we would risk it. "I vote for the safest," I said. Frankie and Eli seconded and thirded the vote.

Fog curled around the mountain, and we couldn't see more than a few feet in front of us. The trail was barely visible with a wall of rocks on one side and a wall of darkness on the other. Eli picked up a pebble and threw it over the side. It cracked against something and kept bouncing before it finally stopped.

Frankie took a step back. "We're going to want to stay far away from the edges."

"This may work to our advantage," I said, and they both looked at me like I had lost my mind. "I mean, think about it. It's foggy out, and there are tons of trails. Nulan and her patrol can't know which one we took if we cover our tracks. They'll have to divide their forces to check each path. And Rovey said that his magic left a mark on us. We only need to stay one step ahead of him until it wears off."

"And this path is so narrow that they'll have to walk in a single-file line," Frankie added. "That should slow them down—assuming that the darkbringers avoid flying in the fog."

"That's looking on the bright side," Eli grumbled. "Miss Safest Route."

Speaking of single-file lines, that was the only way we could traverse the trail, too. At first, the route was okay. It was clear of debris and wide enough to make us almost forget the deadly cliffs below. Frankie and I took turns covering our tracks. She used her energy to smooth out the dirt, and I called forth wind with the staff to do the same. We walked for hours, and my feet hurt more with every step. We came to a part of the path that was not so much a trail as it was a slope with loose rocks.

"There is no way I'm going over that!" Eli protested. "Especially at night."

"He's right, Maya," Frankie said, rubbing her eyes. "We're tired, and we haven't heard anyone following us. Maybe Nulan will wait until morning."

Even if I didn't want to stop, we couldn't climb across the stretch of rocky terrain at night. We couldn't see how far it went even with the light from the staff, which got eaten up by the fog. "But you're right," I conceded. "We'll start again at daybreak."

"Good," Eli said, "because I'm hungry."

Frankie slid down to take a seat beside the rockface. "You're always hungry."

"Hey," Eli said. "I'm a growing boy."

We ate and huddled together against the mountain, too scared to move closer to the edge of the trail. The night was silent except for the occasional howling and wing-beats. Both sounded too close for comfort. I kept imagining Nulan creeping down the side of the mountain to catch us unaware, so I took the first watch.

When morning came, we saw that a chunk of the trail had fallen away, leaving a six-foot gap. No way we'd be able to jump across it, especially not knowing the condition of the rocks on the other side. Every time I looked down at the endless fog, my palms began to sweat.

Eli was off taking care of his business while Frankie paced back and forth. She was nervous too, but she didn't say anything. When Eli returned, she offered him a squirt of her hand sanitizer, which he gladly accepted.

"I have an idea," I said, looking across the gap in the trail again, swearing that it was growing wider by the second. I clutched the staff, hoping I could get it to cooperate. The symbols started to glow and peeled away. They floated in the air around us.

"You can do so much with your magic." Eli let out a deep sigh. "I guess it's like Miss Lucille said . . . my magic is more specialized, which translates to *not that useful in most situations.*"

"I think it's because of the staff," I said, convinced of it. "Remember how Frankie figured out that it was a conduit to channel magic? You should try it one day."

"I might just do that." Eli wiggled his fingers. "I'm sure that I'm destined for greatness."

The staff changed into black sand that sparkled with silver. It swooped from my hand to the mountainside, where it curved across the path. A wood walkway appeared piece by piece. The symbols floated to the platform and burned into it.

"Why does magic always have to be so illogical," Frankie said. "Wood turning to sand then to wood again. Really?"

Eli slapped her on the back, laughing. "Yes, we know, don't Frankiefy us right now, okay?"

I took a step forward. "I'll go first."

"Next," Eli yelled before Frankie could.

She groaned but didn't protest.

The wind whipped through my locs, threatening to pull my hair out of my ponytail. I shouldered my backpack and tightened the straps. It was now or never. I sucked in a breath and set off across the bridge of god symbols. I took one careful step after another, watching my feet. Out of the corner of my eyes, I could see some of the jagged rocks far below. No one could ever hope to survive a fall here, and that thought made me more nervous.

I was halfway across the bridge when it swayed in the wind. Eli had climbed on, and the flimsy wood didn't like the extra weight. The morning dew was settling on the platform, making my sneakers slippery. Eli had made it halfway when Frankie climbed on the bridge, then slipped. It happened in slow motion like a scene in a horror movie playing out frame by frame. She went down hard and rolled over the side of the ledge.

"No," Eli said, running back for her, but that was a mistake. He slipped too and almost fell.

I was running to help when something blue cut across my vision, descending from the sky. I saw a flash of a barbed tail, then I knew it was a darkbringer. He moved in and out of the fog so fast that I didn't see him until he was right there. He crouched against the rockface, peering down at Frankie, who'd managed to grab on to the edge of the wood. He wore all black—like Rovey and his soldiers. My belly flip-flopped.

"Take my hand if you want to live," the darkbringer said, his voice as cold as ice.

Wait. Was he paraphrasing the Terminator? And why was this darkbringer helping us?

Frankie didn't take his hand at first. She slipped some more, and he reached again. This time she grabbed his hand, and he yanked her from the bridge and disappeared into the fog.

"Frankie!" I yelled as her screams echoed against the rocks.

Eli crawled the rest of the way across the bridge, his face

wet with tears. I called the staff back, and it materialized at my side again. Eli pressed his fists hard against his forehead. "The darkbringer took her," he cried. "Just took her . . ."

I stood frozen in place, clutching the staff hard enough to make my hand burn. It happened so fast. "We'll find her," I said, my voice choked.

I dropped my head, feeling tired all over. Frankie couldn't be gone. It was my fault that she'd come to the Dark, and now this was my fault, too. I swiped hard at the tears blurring my eyes, but they kept coming.

Another flash caught my attention, and I snapped up the staff, ready to fight. The darkbringer who'd stolen Frankie landed in the fog in front of me. This time he wasn't alone. Someone else stood shrouded in shadows behind him. I stalked toward the darkbringer, heat burning through my body. My skin glowed with blue light. I was going to make him pay.

TWENTY-THREE

FRIEND OR FOE:
IS THERE REALLY A DIFFERENCE IN THE DARK?

A S SOON AS the darkbringer stepped out of the fog, I cursed under my breath. I was both relieved and dismayed to see it was Zeran, the boy we freed at the camp. He wore a black soldier's uniform, although he didn't seem to have any weapons.

He had skin the color of azure with copper freckles across his nose and cheeks. His beautiful jet-black eyes sparkled in the weak morning light. I blinked, squashing all thoughts about his eyes. *Maya Janine Abeola, get your head right.*

This was such a betrayal. I had kept my end of the bargain. In exchange for information and the map, I'd set him free. How dare he snatch up Frankie like a thief in the night? He was asking for what he had coming to him. A butt whupping.

"Where is she?" Eli demanded through gritted teeth.

"You better start talking now," I said, the staff aglow in my hand.

"Is that any way to treat the person who saved Frankie's life?" the darkbringer asked, his eyes wide as if we'd offended him. "I could've let her fall to her death, then she wouldn't be Frankiefying anyone."

It was never a good thing when your enemy knew more about you than you knew about him. He had to have been following us this entire time.

I took one step toward him. "Listen, Zeran, we're not here to play games. Where's Frankie?"

"Ah, so you know my name. How interesting."

The other person, who I'd mistaken for a darkbringer, coughed and made the grossest hacking sound. I thought they'd spit up a lung or something. "Guys, I swallowed a fly," Frankie said, wobbling out of the fog.

I let out a shaky breath, and Eli laughed as she stumbled over to him. "Isn't there supposed to be protein in flies?"

"Worms have protein." Frankie bent over and threw up.

"Not cool!" Eli said, but he was holding back a snicker. He pulled out his phone to snap a photo, but like the last time we were in the Dark, his battery had gone dead. "Ugh, reason number one why this place sucks. I can't even take embarrassing pictures of my friends."

I glanced around to make sure no other darkbringers lingered above or below us. I couldn't stop thinking about Rovey on the train with Nulan. The enemy of my enemy.

"Why are you here?" I asked, turning my attention back to the darkbringer.

"Obviously, I'm here to help." Zeran gave me a blank stare as if to say I should've figured that out by now. "You saved my life at the camp."

"Um, no thanks," Eli butted in after clearing his throat. "You're our sworn mortal enemy, remember?"

"I'm not your enemy, Eli," Zeran snapped. "You should see that by now."

Frankie wiped her mouth with the back of her hand. "He did save my life."

That was true, but I needed to know why. It wasn't out of the goodness of his heart. He'd been pretty clear with his feelings about godlings at the camp and about my father. "What do you want?"

Zeran quirked an eyebrow. "Are we speaking the same language or what? I said that I wanted to help you."

"Technically, no," Frankie answered. "We're actually

speaking English. Maya used her staff to make a universal translator. It's like in the sci-fi shows when aliens from different planets can understand each other, except we're using magic."

The darkbringer frowned. *"Ang-lish?"*

"Never mind," I said, annoyed. "You've repaid your debt to me by saving my friend. Now leave us alone."

Zeran gazed at me through half-lidded eyes like we were boring him. "I've done more than that."

"What's that supposed to mean?" I asked.

"I'll tell you on the way." Zeran headed up our trail. The nerve. This was our quest. We weren't going to let some stranger boss us around.

We walked behind him single file since the path was so narrow, but we didn't have to like it. His wings, which fluttered against his back, were the same inky color as his eyes and hair. His horns sloped alongside his temples and were a warm shade of brown.

Not going to lie. He was the kind of guy that got all the attention at school. People would flock to him, not even on account that he was blue, but he had that air about him. You know, when you couldn't put your finger on what makes something or someone so appealing.

The darkbringer commander had accused my friends and me of setting his camp on fire—the same fire that had started after I freed Zeran. "You did it, didn't you?" I accused him. "You burned the camp down."

Zeran inhaled a deep breath. He didn't sound proud when he said, "Yes. I did it to keep the commander off your trail. He's a good tracker and would've caught up with you long before you made it to Zdorra if I hadn't."

The trail started to slope downhill as we descended the other side of the mountain. It was hard enough to walk uphill on loose rocks, but downhill was even worse. The three of us kept stumbling and almost losing our footing while Zeran made it look easy. We'd finally made it below the fog, where it was even darker because the mountain blocked out the sunlight.

"That was also me at the rail station," Zeran said after a long pause. I suspected he was concentrating on navigating the trickier parts of the trail too. "When you and Frankie were about to get caught with those stolen E-passes, I set off the alarm to distract the guards."

"Were you also the woman who helped Eli after we got off the train?" I asked.

"No," he said, his voice bored. "I don't know what it's like in the human world, but some people will go out of their way to help others."

"We have the same, duh," Eli whispered to Frankie. "Who does this guy think he is?"

"I covered your tracks to lead COO Nulan and her patrol on a different path up the mountain, too," Zeran added. "You and Frankie did an awful job of it."

"You like bragging about yourself," I said, "but you still haven't answered the real question. Why have you been helping us?"

"I'm not helping you per se." Zeran stopped in his tracks and turned around. "I'm helping myself." He paused, letting that bit of information settle in, but I was even more confused now. "I don't want my people to go to war."

"That's what we're trying to prevent," I admitted, feeling uneasy sharing any information with him.

"I get why our lord wants revenge on the other celestials, but this war is wrong," he continued. "Our world is doing fine now—or it was until he mandated that we prepare for war. It's been going on for hundreds of years." Zeran turned his back to us again. "We're tested when we're ten. If we have desirable powers, we're shipped off to training, even if our parents protest. I tried to run away. Lots of kids do."

"And they were going to send you to the stocks because you didn't want to fight?" I asked, shifting on my heels. "That's just wrong."

Zeran started down the path again. "Yes."

"At the rail station," I said, "we heard people say that

no one comes back from the stocks . . . um . . . right in the head."

Zeran's shoulders stiffened. "You work sixteen-hour days. It's the absolute worst."

"Sounds like corporate America," Eli joked. "Zombies in suits except on Fridays, then it's zombies in jeans."

"Do they put you in a metal collar to neutralize your powers, so you have to do the work without magic?" Zeran sped up, and his steps became less careful. Rocks slid underneath his feet and tumbled over the side of the mountain. "And make you spend your life in forced labor?"

Eli had most definitely missed the mark with his comment. "Um . . . sorry," he apologized. "That's just wrong."

Zeran inhaled a sharp breath and changed the subject. "I'm not the only one who wants to stop a war with your world. People have tried to reason with the Lord of Shadows, but he won't listen. So the only chance I have is to help you, daughter of Elegguá."

I wasn't about to start trusting him on his word alone. As for the war part, it made sense that some of the darkbringers didn't want to fight.

"If you want to help, then tell me how the Lord of Shadows is causing tears in the veil," I demanded.

Zeran slowed down like he was weighing a big decision. "I overheard Rovey saying that the Lord of Shadows had a weapon at the Crystal Palace. I think that it may be the source of the tears." He let out a deep sigh. "That map you got isn't quite what it seems."

"We figured that out already," I said.

"The palace is hidden," Zeran said. "The map will show you endless paths to get there, all treacherous."

"That seems very . . ." I said.

"Diabolic?" Frankie offered.

"So you know how to get to the palace?" I asked.

"Not exactly," Zeran said. "I don't know the route the map will take you on, but my unit trained through many traps you may run into on the way."

I wasn't sure we should trust him. If the Lord of Shadows wanted me alive—*needed me alive*—this could be a trick.

"I'll help you get to the palace so you can prevent the veil from falling," Zeran offered.

"We need to talk it over," I said, crossing my arms. "Alone."

Zeran threw up his hands and stepped over the side of the cliff. After a few seconds, I could hear the sound of his wing beats growing distant in the fog. It was the same sound from last night. I couldn't believe that he'd been following us since the darkbringer camp and we didn't have a clue.

Eli set his jaw, his expression icy. "I don't trust him."

"I'm not sure that his story adds up," Frankie said.

"I don't think he's telling us the whole truth." I bit my lip. "At the same time, I don't believe that every darkbringer wants this war. I mean, who wants to die? Especially a war involving gods. The devastation would be huge."

"What if everything he said was a lie?" Eli stared out aimlessly into the fog. "He could be a spy for Rovey, trying to get back in the commander's good graces after messing up."

"Why go through this trouble if that's the case?" I countered. "He could've attacked us as soon as we let him out of the cage."

Frankie clutched the straps of her backpack. "That's true . . ."

"Should we take a vote?" I suggested.

"Against," both Frankie and Eli said quickly.

"What happened to keep your friends close and your enemies closer?" I asked, hoping they'd reconsider. I wanted to believe the darkbringer. Plus, if the map was leading us into traps, we needed all the help we could get. Usually Frankie was the reasonable one between the three of us, but she crossed her arms. I sighed in defeat. "I guess we'll find out soon enough if he's friend or foe when I tell him we've voted to give him the boot."

"Friend or foe," Eli said. "Is there really a difference in the Dark?"

Wingbeats filled the air as Zeran cut across the sky and landed in front of us, blocking the path. His wings stretched out wide as his tail swept the ground back and forth in agitation.

Zeran put his hands on his hips and tilted his head to the side like he'd designated himself our fearless leader. He shook out his wings, spraying us with a fine mist. Had he done that on purpose?

"Sorry," he said, his cheeks deepening to purple.

A single black feather fell away from his left shoulder. With lightning-fast reflexes, he reached up and caught it. The feather turned into black mist before our eyes. Okay, so he really had this "I'm cooler than you, and I'm going to show you every chance I get" vibe going on for himself. It was equal parts fascinating and annoying.

Zeran looked at the space between Frankie and me. "What did you decide?"

Eli stepped forward with his chest stuck out, attempting to look tougher. He cleared his throat and projected his voice like he was on stage in an auditorium. "Don't take this the wrong way or anything, but we'll pass on your offer to help."

"We appreciate you for saving Frankie," I said, rocking on my heels.

Zeran's jaw dropped, and he burst into laughter. "Oh, this is precious," he spat as he turned to leave. "You're going to be begging for my help. Wait and see." At that, he opened his wings and flew away.

"Well, that's that," Frankie said.

Somehow, I wasn't so sure that was the last we'd see of him.

TWENTY-FOUR

WE GET LOST IN A CREEPY FOREST

I THOUGHT ABOUT ZERAN as we hiked down the mountain. Meeting him and seeing the people in the city only made me more curious about the Dark. What did people do for fun? Did they have comic books? Did they play kickball? Was it wrong that I wanted to know more about them? Zeran had said that he wasn't our enemy. I wanted to believe that was true of most darkbringers.

I pulled out the map, and to no one's surprise, it had changed again. According to it, we only had to get through the forest that had appeared out of nowhere. After that, we'd have to cross another swamp to reach the palace. All told, we should be there in another two or three days if we didn't run into any more trouble. That was too long, so I put the map aside and drew the staff in a circle. "Let's see if we can make a shortcut."

I concentrated on opening a gateway on the other side of the forest, but I could feel something wrong with it. Instead of the usual roaring of the wind, it was dead quiet. It was the same as before when I tried to open a gateway close to my father's soul. The god symbols on the bridge grew dimmer until it faded and the gateway closed.

Frankie hugged her arms to her chest. "More wards?"

"Yeah," I said, frustrated. "I can't break through them."

A sudden static in the air drew my attention away from my umpteenth fail attempt in the Dark at making a gateway. The hairs stood up on my arms. I stared at the sky. It was purple with spots of black bruises, and magic pulled at every fiber of my body. Déjà vu washed over me — the sense of something familiar.

Eli stepped next to me and glanced up, too. "Is that what I think it is?"

"A tear," I said, as black lightning struck between two clouds. It was the same as when I opened gateways. The sparks grew until it stretched into a gaping hole.

I turned circles, crouched with the staff ready, but there was no enemy to fight. The tear had opened by itself. "This can't be happening."

"So, the tears are random on this side of the veil too," Frankie concluded. "That's fascinating."

"Is this one deep enough to cross into our world?" Eli asked.

"Yes," I said, my voice hoarse. How did this tear feel so similar to my gateways, minus the god symbols? I hadn't noticed that on the human side, but now it was obvious. Maybe I could feel it because we were closer to the source of the tears.

"Not to rush you or anything, but we already know the darkbringers can track tears." Eli rubbed the back of his neck, his attention darting to the forest. "You plan on closing this one anytime soon?"

I didn't answer him as I let go of the staff—I *couldn't* answer. I had to make sure that I was right first. The staff stood up on its own before it sprouted wings and turned into a harness. My hand trembled as I slipped it on my back and ascended into the sky. I approached the tear and slowed, coming within inches of it. It hummed against my skin. *PULSE. PULSE. BEEP. PULSE. PULSE. BEEP.* The harmonics of the tear thumped steady, unchanging, taunting.

My vision slipped out of focus, and for a moment, I only saw a flash of white as the world started to tilt. My wings faltered, and I dipped a few feet before catching myself. Eli or Frankie hollered something at me, but it took all my concentration to stay airborne. I squeezed my eyes closed and counted from ten. The dizziness abated after a while, but not soon enough.

I wiped the sweat from my brow and made quick work of closing the tear and rejoined my friends. The staff went back to normal. "We should keep moving," I said, heading into the forest. I saw the way both of them were looking at me, and I didn't want to talk about it.

Within moments, we were deep in a forest so dense that it blocked the sun. Frankie whipped out her flashlight, and the staff grew brighter to help push back the darkness. The trees were lush with broad dark purple leaves and green bark. Somewhere nearby, we could hear the calming roar of a river. I didn't care about any of those things. I stopped and braced myself. My friends deserved to know the truth. "That tear was from godling magic, and before you ask, yes, I'm sure."

"What does that mean?" Frankie said. "It's not like a godling would be helping the Lord of Shadows." She studied my face. "Wait, you have a theory?"

"Some godlings live a long time, don't they?" I told them. "Look at the cranky Johnston twins." I forced out my next words, feeling like I was betraying Papa. "I can feel how similar the magic is to my own. It's almost identical.

As I see it, there are two possibilities to explain why godling magic is causing tears. One, the Lord of Shadows somehow absorbed Eleni's magic when he killed her. Two, she never died, and she's helping him."

"Maya, okay, we can buy the first option, but second, wow, that's cold," Eli said. "You can't believe that your sister would help the man who killed her family."

"*Half sister,*" I corrected him. I massaged my temples. My head was throbbing. "I don't want to believe it's true, but we have to consider it. The Lord of Shadows befriended her on the crossroads—we don't know if he got her to switch sides then."

Neither of them said anything else as we continued deeper into the forest. We tuned in to the rustling of leaves, twigs cracking, and the low whistle of the wind. This one was the most normal forest we'd been through in the Dark, which probably meant we had to stay extra alert. If what Zeran said about the map was true, and it had been so far, then this forest would prove to be another obstacle.

"I don't know how this is possible, but I smell pecan pie," Frankie said, rubbing her belly.

Eli wrinkled his nose. "It smells like armpits and dirty gym socks to me."

When I inhaled, something in the air reminded me of Mama's lilac perfume.

"The top five best places to see a ghost," Eli said, defusing some of the tension between the three of us. "One, a haunted house; two, a haunted cemetery; three, a haunted hotel; four, a haunted, abandoned amusement park; and five, a haunted forest. And we have a winner."

"Can we talk about something else?" Frankie asked as a gust of wind slammed into us.

A scream rang out in the forest, and I froze with my ears perked. *I'm here, Maya,* my father's voice whispered to me. Tears sprang to my eyes. Was Papa here? How was that possible? *Help me, baby girl.*

I shook my head, trying to clear my thoughts. Papa couldn't be here. He was at home in a coma. *The Lord of Shadows trapped my soul in the forest, Maya,* Papa said. *I can't find my way out. Please help me before it's too late.*

Maya, honey, where are you? Mama called. *It's so cold here.*

This was absurd. Mama would never come to the Dark world. Papa wasn't here either. That said, the forest sounded exactly like my parents, which made me think that it was reading my thoughts. What kind of nightmarish thing would it conjure when it knew your hopes and fears? I shuddered and pushed the voices out of my head, trying desperately to ignore them.

"I'm coming, Jayla!" Eli screamed. "Don't move."

"Eli, don't," I yelled as he tunneled through the thick bushes and disappeared.

I looked to where Frankie had been only a minute ago, and my blood went cold. She was gone, too.

TWENTY-FIVE

WHAT COULD BE WORSE THAN HUNGRY SHADOWS?

I TURNED IN A CIRCLE, looking for my friends in the endless trees and overgrown bushes, but they were gone. The forest was dark beyond the light of the staff. I could hear the faint sound of leaves crunching beneath feet, but I couldn't pinpoint the direction. The wind howled and rustled through the grass. It wasn't my imagination that shadows slithered around the edges of the trail. I saw a bobbing light out of the corner of my eyes.

"Frankie!" I called, but the light blinked out, only to reappear in a completely new location. That was impossible. I started to veer off the path to go after the light, but someone grabbed my arm. I swung the staff.

"Hey, slow down," Zeran said as he deflected the blow. "You run off like that, and you won't be able to help them."

"Let go!" I snapped, pulling my staff back from him. "What are you doing here?"

"I heard the screaming—figured you were in trouble again," he said. "I wasn't following you or anything."

"Sure, you weren't," I groaned. "Do you know anything about this forest?"

"All I know is that Command sends every recruit here at some point for training." Zeran squinted as he looked at shadows crawling across bushes near the trail. "It's called the Lost Forest. There's a rumor that a fourth of the recruits who come here don't make it back."

"So convenient that you're here to save the day," I said, rolling my eyes.

Zeran glared at me. "I can't tell if you truly believe that I'm your enemy or if you can't stand not being the hero in every situation."

"Excuse me?" My face felt hot with embarrassment. "Don't mind me. I'm just trying to save both our worlds and my friends right now."

"No." Zeran winced and squeezed his eyes tight. "It can't be him."

"Can't be who?" I asked, dread filling my belly.

Zeran opened his eyes, taking a step in one direction, then in another. He jerked his head around like he heard something, but it was still quiet in the forest. "Billu, is that you?" Tears clouded his dark eyes. "Is it really you, little brother? I'll find you; I promise. You don't have to be scared."

Zeran started to step off the trail, and I grabbed his arm. "No," I said. "Your brother isn't here. It's a trick. I heard my parents earlier."

"How would you know?" Zeran pulled out of my grasp, then he almost fell in a tangle of writhing shadows that had crawled up next to the trail. He blinked twice. "Wait, you're right. Billu can't be here. This must be how the forest gets you."

"Maya, my flashlight went out," Frankie called. "I can't find my way back."

"Frankie," I shouted, relieved to hear her voice, "why did you leave the trail?"

"I heard Mama Pam," she said, but her voice now came from the other side of the forest. "She needed my help."

I stared up at Zeran, whose face looked grim. "I was afraid that would happen. I don't know how, but the forest can move people. That's why people get lost; they're *misplaced*."

"Is Eli with you?" a third Frankie asked from another direction.

One voice had come from my left, another from in front, and the last from behind.

"No, he's lost in the forest, too," I said, worried that he

hadn't called out in all this time. I turned back to Zeran. "We'll have to try the process of elimination to find them."

Several teachers at Jackson Middle were huge fans of the process of elimination. Consider and reject each possible choice until you only had one left. Okay, I had three positions for Frankie, but there was a chance that she wasn't in any of those locations. So I had four choices. That meant that I had a twenty-five percent chance of making the right choice the first time. This was like a standardized test but with impossible stakes.

"Maya, hurry up," Frankie called from behind again. "There are shadows everywhere, just like the night the werehyenas attacked us."

"Keep talking, and we'll look for you, okay?" I hollered back. "Talk about your moms."

"Okay," she answered from behind.

"Where does your mom Dee work?" I asked.

"At the University of Chicago," said her voice from in front of us.

"In the department of biomolecular research," answered the third, somewhere to our left.

My head was spinning. We would be lost in this forest forever at this rate.

"Not to interrupt your riveting conversation," Eli called out, "but can we get out of here already?" He sounded winded, like he was on the run. I imagined him darting through the forest, whipping through grass, completely invisible.

Eli popped out of the bushes covered in dirt, his clothes torn. He'd sounded so far away seconds ago. I breathed a sigh of relief as I slapped him on the shoulder. To my horror, something lashed out at my hand. Eli gave me a devious smile before his form shifted into a black mass of writhing shadows. The shadows grew taller and taller. Ribbons shot out and wrapped around my wrists like chains. My staff hit the ground. Ice crystals crawled up my arms as I struggled to free myself.

"Let her go." Zeran rammed his fist straight into the wall of shadows. White cracks spread from the place that Zeran had landed his punch and began to spread. It was like watching glass shattering in slow motion. Pieces of the shadows began to fall to the ground and retreat. The shadows screeched, and other horrible, bloodcurdling screams came from all around us.

"We'll have to check each direction one by one," Zeran said before he took a few steps and propelled himself into the sky. The wind from his wings whipped through my braids. I grabbed my staff and set off running behind him. I cut through the tall grass, knocking away vines that snapped at my ankles.

A shadow pounded me across my back, and I hit the ground hard. The staff landed a few feet away, still glowing. I reached out my hand, and it flew toward me, but another shadow snatched it right out of the air. I watched in disbelief as the shadow snapped my staff.

"No," I screamed as the two halves landed in the dirt. The light faded from the god symbols. My body felt like it was on fire as I climbed to my feet. Blue light pulsed across my forearms. "You really shouldn't have messed with my friends or my staff."

I gritted my teeth and ran straight toward another wall of shadows, which wasn't my smartest move. When we collided, the impact knocked me on my butt, but something else happened too. A white light began to snake through the shadows, tearing holes in the darkness. The shadows screeched again, but this time, they didn't break apart. The light kept growing until it swallowed the shadows whole.

"Argh!" Zeran screamed.

I grabbed the two halves of my staff and sprinted toward his voice. Maybe he would be in a new location by the time I got there, but I didn't have time for these games. I had to find Papa's soul before it was too late. I had to save my friends. I would get out of this forest if I had to fight every single shadow by myself.

"Can someone explain to me why shadows are trying to eat us?" Eli asked from somewhere near the same location as Zeran.

"We've already established that they aren't exactly friendly," Frankie said.

I swallowed my hope, knowing that the forest was a trickster. When I got to the clearing, though, I found Frankie and Eli tangled in shadows. I had no time to celebrate. A shadow had Eli by the foot and was dragging him deeper into the forest. Frankie had lassoed her energy magic around his waist and was pulling him back with all her might.

Zeran was fighting three shadow monsters on his own, but they had him surrounded. They lashed out at him, and shards of ice crystallized against his skin. He held his own until one of the shadows flung him to the ground. He didn't move as the three descended upon him like he was helpless prey.

"I got Eli," Frankie shouted through gritted teeth. "Help Zeran."

Frankie was holding on to the energy rope with both hands, and then she let it go. I gasped and for one brief, terrifying moment, I thought Eli was a goner. Frankie launched a mini energy disk. It sliced through the air and cut the shadow right below Eli's sneaker. If she'd been a few inches off, she would have hit him.

Eli flopped on his back. "I'm going to pass out now."

I was on top of the shadows attacking Zeran before they saw me coming. Both parts of the staff glowed in my hands. I slammed the sticks into the shadows hard. The impact vibrated up my arms into my teeth. My vision was a blur as I twisted and turned to keep out of their grasp. The shadows screamed as white veins of white started to form around the places that my sticks struck. After enough hits, they fled deeper into the forest.

"Thank you," Zeran said. "I guess I owe you my life again."

I reached out a hand to help him up. He looked at me sideways before taking it. "You don't owe me anything. Thanks for coming back to help us."

Zeran stood up to his full height and shook off the ice crystals from his arms and wings. "Don't mention it."

Frankie helped Eli to his feet. They fist-bumped, then added in an elbow tap for good measure.

"Take that, shadows," Eli cheered. "We didn't come here to play with y'all. We're the League of Godlings and one butt-kicking darkbringer."

"How are we going to get back to the trail?" Frankie asked.

"Leave that to me." Zeran brushed dirt from his uniform. "I have an impeccable sense of direction."

I sighed, expecting as much. "Of course you do."

It turned out that he wasn't exaggerating, either. He got us back on the trail in less than ten minutes.

"We better get out of here before they decide to come back," Zeran suggested.

"Ghosts, I'm okay with," Eli proclaimed, "but I am not at all into hungry shadows."

I kept eyes on the edges of the trail, looking for more shadows. "I wish that we could've have gone around the forest, even if it was by foot."

"As I understand and from everything we've seen, that's not how the map works," Frankie said. "You have to go on the path that it sets for you to get to the Crystal Palace."

Zeran grinned, much to Eli's and my annoyance. "Finally, someone's listening to me."

"This time we stay on the trail." I pressed the two parts of my staff back together. There was a flash of bright light from the impact, but then the staff was as good as new. Relief rushed through me. In truth, I'd gotten used to having it around.

"I'll put up a shield," Frankie said, as her magic sparked to life on her fingertips.

We started down the trail again. More shadows closed in around us, but this time we were ready.

TWENTY-SIX

AS LUCK WOULD HAVE IT, WE BECOME FOOD

W E STUMBLED OUT of the forest on blistered feet, tired and dirty, and out of food. I shielded my eyes from the weak sunlight as I leaned on the staff. Frankie braced her hands against her knees to take a breather. I almost pointed out that she had leaves stuck in one of her puffy pigtails, but Eli said something first. We wouldn't have made it out of the forest in one piece if Frankie hadn't used her shield to protect us from the shadows. When she got tired, Zeran and I took point.

I finally understood what had happened on our field trip at school. Before, I thought the writhing ribbons that somehow crossed into our world belonged to the Lord of Shadows. But it wasn't him. It was shadows like the ones in the forest that had weaved around the dinosaurs at the Field Museum. The Lord of Shadows had sent them as a reminder and a warning that he was coming to destroy our world. He knew they would strike fear in the hearts of celestials and godlings alike.

We trudged forward, and it felt like we'd spent days in the forest. What if I was too late? No, I couldn't think that way. Papa would hold on a little longer. He would be okay, and together we would figure out how to stop the Lord of Shadows from tapping into the veil. Still, I couldn't get rid of that sinking feeling in my belly that I was already out of time.

"Tell us about yourself," Frankie asked Zeran as we continued following the map. "How did you end up in the army?"

"Command sends soldiers to schools to test us when we're ten, and I caught their attention," he said, his face hard. "I tried to hide my magic, but they're good at getting what they want."

I thought of the standardized tests that we had to do this year. That was bad enough, but drafting kids into an army to start a war was far worse.

"If it were just me, I wouldn't care so much, but my little brother Billu can do incredible things with his powers." Zeran flushed a deeper purple—not only his cheeks, but his whole body turned violet. "Command took him away two months ago, and I left the army to join the Resistance. They said that they could help me get him back. I have to save my brother before Command makes him use his powers to hurt someone."

"I'm sorry that happened to you and your brother," I said, rocking on my heels. I wanted to ask him what sort of things his little brother could do, but this was not the time. "How are you going to find him now?"

"Billu is at the Crystal Palace, where the most talented recruits go," Zeran explained. "I'm coming with you to get him back."

"Sounds to me like the Lord of Shadows is due for a beat down." Eli cracked his knuckles. "If it were my little sister, I'd take out his whole crew to rescue her."

Zeran exchanged a smile of solidarity with Eli. "So you think a godling is helping the Lord of Shadows destroy the veil? I may have been eavesdropping on your conversation the other day."

"Yeah," I mumbled, still not quite believing it myself. "Have you seen one who, um, looks a little like me?"

"I don't remember anyone ever mentioning a godling here before you three came a few months ago," said Zeran.

That should've been a relief to hear, but I still didn't have a good feeling about it. I would find out soon enough if

Eleni had been helping the Lord of Shadows. "Why haven't more darkbringers gone through the tears?"

"Oh, they have," Zeran confirmed. "The Lord of Shadows only sends the ones who can shift their appearance and act human. Their mission is to infiltrate your world and learn how to exploit your weaknesses."

Dread coursed through my chest. This was my fault. I was supposed to help protect the veil, and darkbringers had slipped into our world already. I didn't know why this was such devastating news, when we'd fought darkbringers twice in the human world. But hearing that they had snuck into our world and were hiding right under our noses scared me. Neither Papa nor the orisha council had said anything to suggest that they even knew about it.

My hands shook as I studied the map. The Crystal Palace looked to be another half day's journey away if the course didn't change again. "We can get to the palace tomorrow." I bit my chapped lips. Yes, we'd make it there, but we were in no shape to fight if it came down to it, which it would. We had to come up with a plan.

"I hear a river," Frankie said, perking up.

My mouth and throat were so dry. "I hate to admit this," I groaned, "but we're not going to storm any castles in our current condition. We need water and to find some food."

Frankie and Eli looked to Zeran, who threw up his hands. "I'm a terrible hunter."

"But are you an okay fisherman?" I asked, quirking an eyebrow.

"At the very least, you can tell us what we can and can't eat," Frankie said.

"Oh, am I supposed to be the nature boy because I grew up in the Dark?" Zeran rolled his eyes. "Let me whip out my handy guidebook so I can tell you which mushrooms aren't poisonous. Guess what? They're all poisonous. Some will cause your eyeballs to bleed, and others will make your belly bloat until it bursts."

Eli slapped Zeran on the back. "Good thing we have our resident darkbringer to the rescue."

When we found the river, we drank and refilled our water bottles. After that, we scrubbed our arms and faces and washed off the last of the blue paint from our skin. Stealth mode was officially over.

"Why didn't you change yourself to look like us instead of wearing those silly outfits?" Zeran asked as he squatted beside the river, trying to weave some leaves into a fishing net.

I blinked at him in disbelief. "We can't just do that. Can you?"

Zeran nodded. "I was top in my transformation class three years in a row."

"We can see you didn't win any awards for net weaving, though," Eli teased him.

"I'd work a lot faster if you weren't staring as me the whole time," Zeran shot back.

"We'll give you some space," I said.

Speaking of class, I wondered how the new godlings at Jackson Middle were doing at school. Ogun would be training kids to control their magic, but were the cranky twins still there, too? They had quite the mess to clean up at the Field Museum and lots of memories to erase.

"You know." Eli poked out his lips and nodded. "I kind of like him—Zeran, I mean. I'm not saying I trust him yet, but he's cool."

"He's okay, I guess," I said, and Frankie blushed.

We surveyed the area and found a small grove of trees behind some boulders. Glowing golden fruit hung in clusters from the branches between plump green leaves. I had to stop myself from squealing with joy. We'd finally found food.

"OMC!" Eli drooled. When I cocked an eyebrow at him, he added, "OMC, as in *oh my celestials!*"

"We should wait until Zeran gets here to make sure it's okay," I said, but Eli ignored me. He plucked one of the fruits, which looked like a cross between an apple and a pear.

He turned it over in his hand. "What is it with the Dark and their glowing food?"

I remembered then that we'd landed in a field with glowing purple corn the first time we'd come to the Dark. Eli had a point.

"Maya's right; we should wait—" Frankie started to say, but it was too late. Eli bit into the fruit. Juice filled the corners of his mouth, and he moaned in delight. "It sort of tastes like a kiwi without the seeds."

Frankie plucked one of her own and lifted it to her nose. "It smells nauseatingly sweet."

Zeran rushed into the grove, cutting through the bushes and vines at a dead sprint. Sweat streaked down his forehead. "Nulan and the city patrol are headed this way," he said, out of breath. Before any of us could respond, he spotted the fruit in Frankie's hand. "Don't eat that." He frowned. "It's dangerous."

Eli spat out the half-chewed pulp. "Um . . . what did you say?"

"Oh, no." Zeran massaged his temples. "That's jeejee fruit. Its sole purpose is to feed the grove."

"What do you mean feed?" Eli dropped the fruit. It hit the ground and rolled a few feet away. "Tell me that doesn't mean what it sounds like."

"The jeejee tree is a predator," Zeran explained. "The

fruit will lure anyone who eats it into a deep sleep. If they're unlucky enough to nap here, the ground then absorbs them while they're out cold. I don't know how that works exactly, but that's the story."

"The Dark is such a charming place," Eli groaned. "Everything wants to eat you."

"Blame that on Elegguá." Zeran glanced over my shoulder, his face in a deep frown. "The legends say that when he split the earth, it transformed the Dark in ways that were not natural. Simple harmless trees and animals became more deadly."

Everyone was looking at me, and I didn't know what to say. Papa had made a mistake with the veil. He'd paid the price, but so had the people of the Dark. Sometimes mistakes happened and they could be fixed, and sometimes we had to live with them and vow to do better.

"I'm sorry," I said, my voice shaking. "He didn't mean to do that."

"You don't have to apologize for your father, Maya." Zeran sighed and his expression softened a little. "We know the history of the world. He did it to protect the seeds of humanity. Besides, more people died during our wars against the orishas than anything else."

"Still, I wish none of this had happened," I insisted, feeling guilty.

"We need to go," Zeran said. "Nulan isn't far behind.

Eli do you think you can—" Before Zeran finished his sentence, Eli had curled up on the ground, fast asleep.

Frankie put her hands on her hips. "He has the worst timing."

"Can we wake him?" I said.

Zeran grimaced, shaking his head. "Not for a few hours, at least." Then he frowned at Frankie. "Can you create a force field for two for a few minutes?"

"Yes!" she answered.

"If you lie on the ground with Eli, the grove will draw you inside the earth . . ."

The dirt had already started to move around Eli like a sleeping giant waking up.

"Ah, that's clever." Frankie bounced on her heels. "You want me to hide Eli inside the grove and use the force field to stop the earth from eating us."

"Exactly," Zeran exclaimed. "Think you can do it?"

"On it!" Frankie curled up beside Eli. The ground sank faster and swallowed them in seconds. Frankie's energy bubble flared to life before the dirt completely covered them.

"I can give you a disguise," Zeran told me. "It'll only last a few minutes, but that should be enough if Nulan doesn't stick around. We have to make ourselves as uninteresting as possible."

"Okay, do it," I said, hearing the rustling of feet against the leaves nearby. I squeezed the staff and it flashed, turning into a ring again, which I slipped on my finger. If Zeran was planning to betray us, he would've done it by now and with a lot less stepping in to play hero. He'd put his life on the line to save Frankie from falling off the cliff, then again to rescue us in the forest.

Zeran touched my cheek, his hand warm against my skin. My face started to vibrate and change shape. My legs grew longer. My locs turned from black to neon green, and my skin morphed from brown to blue.

"Whoa, this is pretty awesome," I said. Even my voice had grown deeper. "How did you do that?"

Zeran scratched his head, blushing deep purple again. He'd changed his appearance, too. His black horns grew larger and curved away from his face. His eyes turned to an eerie silver, and his teeth became pointy fangs. "I'll teach you one of these days if we survive." He brushed the sleeve of my shirt, and my outfit shifted into a dirty mirror of his own — a black soldier's uniform.

As an ominous fog rolled into the grove, Zeran gave me a look that said what I already knew: *they were here.* I drew in a breath as patrol officers surrounded us. Their dark gray uniforms blended in with the fog, so it was hard to figure out how many had come. I toyed with the ring on my pinky finger, itching to feel my staff in my hands again.

"Halt!" someone yelled, and we jumped apart.

The officers had their silvery-blue prods, which crackled

with electric currents. I wouldn't soon forget how one of those weapons had knocked Eli out. The darkbringers themselves ranged from the deepest blues to the deepest purples. Some had barbed tails and horns, and others had wings. Some had all three — a barbed tail, horns, and wings. It was weird to think about this right now, but I'd gotten used to how different they looked from humans. Different wasn't the problem. The problem was that they wanted to destroy the human world. The patrol officers all had one thing in common: they stared at us with their prods raised to strike on command.

"State your name, rank, and unit," came a voice that raked across my ears like claws.

I dug my nail under the ring as Chief of Order Nulan's brown face appeared in the fog. I held my breath, afraid that even with my modifications, she'd recognize me.

Zeran rattled off names, ranks, and a unit without missing a beat.

"Where are your ID chips, *junior grades?*" Nulan asked, stepping closer.

Zeran stood straight with his shoulders back. "We lost them in the forest."

Nulan grabbed his chin and forced him to look at her. "And your unit," she said, her voice so calm that you wouldn't have known that she was a cold-blooded killer. "Where are they?"

"Don't know, sir," Zeran said as her nails pinched into his skin. He showed no signs of being afraid of her. "We've been stuck in the Lost Forest for days—just managed to get out this morning."

"Check him for illusions." Nulan waved to another officer, who thrust his prod into Zeran's side. I clenched my teeth as his legs gave out and he crumbled to the ground. Blood ran out of his nose, but he only grumbled through the pain as he wiped his face. "You appear to be one of us." Nulan moved to stand in front of me. Her golden eyes flashed with contempt like she could already see through my disguise. "Do you have a tongue, girl?"

"Yes, sir!" I glanced at the half-eaten jeejee fruit discarded on the ground. "I have a tongue."

Nulan quirked a plucked eyebrow at me. "Did you both eat from this grove?"

"Yes, sir," I repeated like a robot through gritted teeth. "There's plenty to share."

"Check her," Nulan commanded, and I looked to Zeran, desperate. He'd said to trust him, but I nudged the ring down my finger into the palm of my hand just in case.

The jolt of electricity hit me as soon as the patrol officer jabbed the prod into my side. My whole body seized, and my knees buckled. The ring slipped out of my hand as I hit the ground.

I glared up at Nulan. If she was going to get the best of

me, it wouldn't be with me cowering at her feet. I gagged at the taste of blood on my tongue. Magic rippled across my skin. It pulled and twisted and stretched until the tingling passed. Sweat stung my eyes, and I drew in a sharp breath.

"It's not them." Nulan glowered, clearly disappointed. "Move out." As she turned to go, she added, "It's rather unfortunate that you ate that fruit. Jeejee patches digest their prey for weeks. They excrete an enzyme that keeps you alive as they do. It's a rather painful death."

"What . . . We didn't know," Zeran said, his voice suddenly squeaky. "Can you help us?"

"I could, but I won't," the aziza answered, her iridescent wings fluttering at her back.

She and her patrol officers moved away as Zeran and I pretended to be sleepy. We collapsed to the ground, and moments later, the soil swallowed us whole. This was not part of the plan.

TWENTY-SEVEN

We stumble upon a graveyard

Z ERAN'S WINGS SPREAD WIDE as he shot up from the ground with me in tow. He kept one arm wrapped around my waist as we soared through the air. That was until he clipped a tree branch and got tangled in the leaves. He lost his hold on me, and I plunged toward the grove with a bunch of jeejee fruit to brace my fall. I *might* have (and that's a big might) let out an undignified squeal. By some miracle, Zeran grabbed my arm right before I hit the ground.

"Um, thanks for saving our butts again," I said as he let me down in one piece. I looked for the ring and found it pulsing with light on a pile of leaves. When I picked it up, it turned back into a staff with a deep sigh of indignation.

"I owe you an apology for some of the things I said back

at camp when we first met." Zeran stared at his black boots caked in mud. "I had some ideas about humans and god- lings that weren't true. The Lord of Shadows said that you were all selfish and couldn't be trusted, but you three aren't like that."

"You don't have to apologize," I said, digging my heels into the dirt. "Before we met you, we'd only run into dark- bringers trying to kill us. We thought you were all mindless cronies."

"Mindless cronies, huh?" Zeran finally looked up from his feet, smiling.

I crossed my arms and laughed. "Yup."

"I'm glad we were both wrong," he said.

"Me too." Okay, I'll admit it. Zeran was cute in that dark, brooding way you saw in movies and comic books. It usually didn't work in real life, except it totally worked for him. "I can't believe your magic fooled Nulan and their fancy equipment."

Zeran wriggled his eyebrows. "I did say that I was top in my class."

***

After the ordeal with Nulan, Zeran and I dug through the soil until we reached the edge of Frankie's force field. As soon as she let go of the bubble, Eli's snores filled the air. Frankie let out a deep sigh, and I shook my head.

"Ugh," Eli said, rubbing his belly the next morning.

"Why did you let me eat that jeejee fruit? I have the worst stomachache now—and I had the weirdest dream that I was buried alive."

"We did try to warn you," Frankie said.

"Next time, try harder," Eli insisted.

"Are they always like that?" Zeran whispered to me.

"Yup," I nodded as we trekked through a murky bog that smelled like two-day-old farts. Air pockets bubbled up on the surface of the mud and popped, which only made the smell much worse. The sky had grown darker over the past hour, and the thick clouds were the color of indigo. Streaks of black lightning cut across the sky, and I swallowed hard. Sometimes black lightning appeared right before a tear in the veil. I hoped this wasn't one of those times.

According to the map, we had a straight shot to the palace from here. In a few hours, we'd have to face the Lord of Shadows. It made me queasy to think about being within a hundred feet of him. If he wanted me alive, then it had something to do with the veil. I couldn't think of any other reason. One thing was for sure. The Lord of Shadows hadn't found a way to get through the veil even with Eleni helping him all these centuries. So he'd come up with another scheme—one that involved me.

We still didn't have a plan to defeat him and steal back my father's soul. I didn't even know what a soul looked like.

Before, when we rescued my father, I could feel his presence. I hoped it would be the same with his soul.

Crossing this bog was like walking through wet cement. Mud clung to my jeans, and I struggled to take each step. This was slowing us down, which I bet was the map's reason for bringing us on this path. "Any idea of what we'll be up against at the palace?" I asked Zeran.

"I don't know for sure," he said, sloshing through the bog. "I heard a rumor that the Lord of Shadows has a hundred recruits and twice as many soldiers on the palace grounds."

"Three hundred darkbringers against four," Frankie noted, up to her ankles in mud. "Those are horrible odds."

"There has to be a way to get around the wards," I said. "If so, I could open a gateway inside the palace undetected. That way, we could avoid most of the soldiers altogether."

Eli groaned, with an arm wrapped around his belly. He didn't look so good. His face was paler than usual, and he walked with his shoulders hunched. I was starting to worry about him.

"Let's think about this for a moment." Frankie wrinkled her nose after another air bubble popped right in front of her. "Wards keep people out — sort of like my electromagnetic field. Once you're inside the palace, you might be able to open a gateway without any problems."

"That's a big *might*," I said, waving away the funky smell. "Plus we have to get inside the palace first."

"Does anyone else feel like we're being watched?" Eli asked, glancing around.

Zeran frowned. "I haven't heard or seen anything to suggest that anyone else is out here."

"Me neither," I said, but an eerie thick fog had rolled over the bog. We couldn't see more than a few feet around us at any given time.

"I'm telling you." Eli wiped beads of sweat from his forehead. "We're not alone. I can feel it."

Zeran cracked a lopsided smile and shook his head. "You're just spooking yourself out, Eli. If the city patrol or the soldiers had caught up with us, they would've attacked by now, especially since we're at a disadvantage, stuck in mud and all."

I didn't sense anyone in the fog, but the map was a trickster. First, it had led us straight to Chief of Order Nulan. Then it put us on a treacherous pass that almost got Frankie killed. Who could forget the Lost Forest, with its vicious shadows, or the grove that tried to eat us alive? But above all those things, I trusted Eli's instincts. If he said someone was following us, then I believed him.

"We'll keep a lookout." I tightened my grip on the staff.

Air pockets grew on the surface of the mud and popped at irregular intervals. Except for that and our sneakers sloshing through the mud, it was dead quiet. No mosquitos buzzed around our faces, no wind rustled in the trees, no sound of any animals at all.

Several air pockets popped at once, and the mud let out a collective growl. I stepped on something that cracked underneath my foot. "What was that?" I said, reaching down to pick it up. My hand shook as I stared in shock at the row of teeth covered in mud.

"Is that a mandible?" Frankie asked, pointing a shaky finger at the teeth.

I remembered the model of a skeleton in the corner of Mr. Jenkins's science class. I was pretty sure that I was holding the bottom half of somebody's jaw. I dropped the mandible. "We need to pick up the pace and get out of here."

"Too late," whispered a sinister voice on the wind that set ice in my veins.

"Who said that?" Frankie asked, sparks of electricity growing on her fingertips.

Bones started to rise to the surface of the mud: a skull, a rib cage, a thigh bone, and whole skeletons. My heart thundered against my chest as the truth hit me at once. "This is a graveyard."

"Time to die," growled the man who stepped out of the fog.

The darkbringer was seven feet tall. He wore black cargo pants and a bloodstained black jacket—a soldier's uniform. His whole body had a gray tint to it, and he was *see-through.*

"This can't be possible," Zeran gasped next to me. "That's General Dekala. He's a legend, and he's also been dead for over a hundred years."

"He's a ghost," Eli said, his voice somber. "They all are."

"What does he want—" Before I could get all the words out, I saw the rest of them.

Hundreds of ghastly faces appeared in the fog. Most of them wore soldier uniforms. They were young, old, winged, and horned, and their eyes burned black like pools of hot tar. They all talked at once until the man Zeran called Dekala raised a hand to silence them.

General Dekala smiled, revealing an endless black hole for a mouth. "Goodbye, trespassers, or should I say welcome, for you will never leave this place again."

As the ghosts rushed forward, Frankie raised a force field around us, but they charged through it. She dropped the force field and started to hit the ghosts with balls of energy. That didn't slow them down either. The symbols on my staff lit up as I swung at a ghost who was wielding a battleax. I ducked in time to keep my head, but my staff went straight through him.

"Maya, the staff!" Eli called as he dodged a blow of his own. "I have an idea."

I figured that Eli would've turned invisible by now, but

maybe that didn't work against ghosts. As much as I didn't want to part ways with the staff, I tossed it to him. If he had an idea, that was better than having a tombstone that read *Maya Janine Abeola, death by ghost in a stinky bog.*

Eli caught the staff in one hand. As soon as he did, the symbols pulsed with blue light. New symbols appeared on the staff—symbols that I didn't recognize. They configured themselves in a new pattern, too. "Stop!" Eli shouted, and his voice was the crack of a whip.

The ghosts froze in place as blue light lifted from Eli's skin and spread over the bog. They struggled against his magic, grimacing and glaring at him, but they couldn't move. Even General Dekala had frozen in place. Eli was shaking, and his nose started to bleed.

"Eli," Frankie said, her voice quiet.

He wiped away the trickle of blood from his nose with the back of his hand and gave her a sheepish smile. "Say hello to my new ghost army."

TWENTY-EIGHT

WE BREAK INTO THE CRYSTAL PALACE

I COULDN'T BELIEVE what I was seeing. These were ghosts, as in spirits, as in the undead. Eli was right; ghosts existed! He had a crooked grin on his face, but his whole body shook from the effort of holding the ghosts in place. Frankie sloshed through the mud to be by his side as he leaned on the staff.

"Let go of us, little mutant boy," General Dekala demanded, sounding ticked off.

"Hey, who are you calling mutant?" Eli shot back.

"What are you?" General Dekala asked, and the other ghosts whispered among themselves.

"A human?" Eli rolled his eyes. "Well, actually a god-ling."

"A godling, here?" Dekala scoffed. "Things have changed

since my day if a godling can walk free in the Dark. What has happened? Don't tell me that the veil has finally fallen. That would be a shame."

I couldn't believe that this darkbringer general was against the veil failing, too. I had to remind myself that not everyone in the Dark agreed with what the Lord of Shadows was doing. They didn't want a war with the human world either. "It hasn't failed yet, but it will if we don't stop the Lord of Shadows."

"We need your help getting into the Crystal Palace," Eli blurted out, straight to the point.

"We should eat them," someone hollered from the crowd of ghosts.

"You don't want to eat me," Eli retorted. "I taste as bad as this bog smells."

Several of the ghosts gagged.

Zeran looked at General Dekala with wide eyes. "You challenged the Lord of Shadows for control of the Dark."

"And I got my whole squadron killed for my efforts," the general growled. "The Lord of Shadows tied our spirits to this bog for all eternity as punishment. Now we spend our days waiting for visitors so we can add their souls to our collective misery."

"That's horrible," Frankie said, giving him a stern look. "Both being trapped here and trapping others."

General Dekala shrugged. "Everyone knows the bog's

haunted, so we haven't had a visitor in fifty years. It was boring around here until you came."

"You fought the Lord of Shadows when no one else would," Zeran exclaimed. "You're a legend."

Was it just me, or was Zeran a little starstruck?

"Seems to me that you're standing against him now." General Dekala yawned. "Good luck."

"But we need your help," Eli insisted. "It's fate that I found you . . . You were *meant* to help us."

"*Meant* to help the likes of you?" Dekala crossed his arms. "I may not agree with the Lord of Shadows, but I'm no friend to godlings, either."

Even if General Dekala and his ghost army offered to help, I didn't know if we could trust them, but Frankie was right. Three hundred against four were horrible odds.

"The Lord of Shadows is preparing for war with the other celestials again," Zeran said, his eyes desperate. "When he's done, there'll be nothing left of our people or the Dark."

Dekala ignored Zeran, and Eli waved his arm dismissively. "Let him and his squadron spend another hundred years in this stinky bog."

Eli and Frankie started to slosh through the mud again while the ghosts stood still, locked in place by his magic. I followed, and Zeran reluctantly fell into step with me.

"To think I was going to free them from their eternal prison," Eli grumbled under his breath.

"Wait!" General Dekala shouted. "Do you have the strength to free us, godling?"

I held back a smile. My friend had dropped the one thing the ghosts couldn't resist.

"Oh, now you want to talk, huh?" Eli said, still walking. "Naw, we're done with you."

"We can help you get into the Crystal Palace," Dekala offered.

Eli stopped in his tracks, his back to the general. "We're listening."

"I'm no traitor," Dekala spat out, "but we'll help you get into the palace, and then you'll be on your own after that. I'll do it to protect my people from war, nothing more."

Eli stroked his chin. "My friends and I will confer."

Frankie, Eli, and I moved in for the huddle, but Zeran looked at us, unsure. I waved him over, and he joined us with our arms dragged over each other's shoulders. "What do you think?" Frankie asked. "We do need help."

"General Dekala was the one who started the Resistance," Zeran explained. "If he says he'll help us, we can trust him."

"They already tried to kill us once," I reminded them. "Like, only five minutes ago."

"I'm not holding them anymore, and they haven't attacked again." Eli rubbed his forehead. "This isn't going to make sense, but I believe him. I have this weird connection to the ghosts. It's hard to explain."

"I don't know if we have much choice, Maya," Frankie said, and all three of them—she, Eli, and Zeran—looked to me for a decision.

I sucked in a deep breath. As much as I wanted to say no, this was the distraction we needed to get into the palace. I bit my lip and gave my answer. "Okay."

Once we'd settled it, Eli turned to the ghosts. "We will accept your offer. I'll free you from this bog in exchange for you helping us break into the Crystal Palace."

Dekala nodded, and the squadron broke into chatter. They really wanted out of this bog—not that I blamed them for that. "Call for us when you're ready."

Dekala and the other ghosts faded bit by bit until they disappeared. Eli looked to me, Frankie, then Zeran and grinned. "I got myself a real ghost army." He did a little dance that involved waving his elbows around like chicken wings.

"And I have an idea to get rid of Nulan," I said. "I'll tell you on the way."

Three hours later, we hid in the forest outside of the gate that surrounded the Crystal Palace. It was almost nightfall, and a blanket of shadows shrouded most of it from view.

Five towers of varying heights stretched into the sky. Glass shaped like fish scales covered their bases, while the tops were sharp needle points. To my horror, giant green serpents slithered up the length of the towers. I swallowed hard, hoping we didn't have to go anywhere near those creatures to retrieve my father's soul. The palace itself was sprawling with black stone walls almost completely masked in the fog. The ground was immaculate, with a garden bursting with pristine flower beds. Writhing moss wrapped around the tree branches, and vines snaked between the bars of the ten-foot wrought-iron gate.

Eli lay on his belly in the bushes to my left. "Are those giant snakes?"

To my right, Frankie straightened her glasses. "They are definitely giant snakes."

As we waited for our plan to unfold, we gnawed on berries that Zeran had found after we left the bog. I was too nervous to eat, but we needed to keep up our energy. Zeran squatted nearby and never took his eyes off the palace. He watched the junior recruits run drills behind the gate. He kept searching face after face, looking for his brother.

"Do you see him?" I asked.

Zeran's shoulders slumped. "Not yet, but he has to be in there. I know it."

"You'll find him," I said, hoping that his little brother was okay. "Remember: distract and divide."

"Give me a few minutes." Zeran climbed to his feet. "That's all I'll need." He disappeared into the trees.

Eli squeezed my staff as he entered ghost mode. "Here we go."

Zeran emerged from another part of the forest. I cringed as he called out to the palace. "Hey, is there anyone home?" he said in my voice. "I'm here to get my father's soul back."

I blinked several times. It was weird seeing Zeran pretending to be me. He had locs that swept just past his shoulders, the staff, and even my limited-edition Oya backpack. Did I really sound that whiny? I was going to have to work on that.

When Zeran got closer to the gate, a light shimmered around the whole palace. The air teemed with magic, and I wondered if that was the ward that had stopped me from opening a gateway here.

Here was the plan. If the Lord of Shadows wanted me, then we would make him work for it. Right on cue, soldiers in black uniforms and patrol officers in gray swarmed the grounds. The junior recruits moved so that they were behind the senior soldiers. Dozens more flew up to the ledges around the five crystal towers to take point.

"Bet you can't catch me," Zeran yelled as the backpack melted away and he sprouted purple wings instead. *Nice touch,* I thought, not that I was paying attention. He shot into the sky—a blur of brown and purple.

Nulan appeared from out of nowhere. She pushed through the crowd and swung open the gate. "Leave the godling to me!" Her iridescent wings fluttered against her back, and she launched into the sky after him. I swallowed hard. He had to make sure she didn't catch him for this to work.

"Now!" Eli shouted, squeezing my staff.

Dekala and his ghosts rose from the ground—hundreds of them, gray and in tattered clothes. Some had a missing eye or limb, or blood dripping between their teeth. They moaned and wailed. The soldiers and patrol officers looked terrified at the sight of the ghosts. Had I not known the plan, I'd have been scared too. When Dekala glanced over his shoulder at Eli, I worried that the ghosts would turn on us, but they kept their word.

The ghosts rushed the wrought-iron gate and swarmed the palace grounds. The soldiers and patrol officers fought back, but the ghosts quickly overtook them. Frankie, Eli, and I ducked inside the gate. We moved around the edges of the grounds to stay away from the fighting. I concentrated hard, but I couldn't feel the ward that had blocked me from opening a gateway outside of the palace. So it was true. The ward only stopped someone from entering the palace grounds using magic. It didn't work once we were already inside.

"No turning back," I said as the first sparks appeared in

the air in front of me. Now it was time to open a gateway that would get us closer to my father's soul.

"Ready," said Eli.

Frankie's hands crackled with energy. "Flying giant snakes at twelve o'clock!"

I did a double-take. The green serpents that had been peacefully slithering up the towers soared through the sky, headed straight for us. It was definitely time to go.

My knees were shaking as the three of us entered the gateway side by side. It was pitch-black, and the spinning god symbols on the walkway pulsed with a weak light. The hairs stood up on the back of my neck. This didn't feel right. We landed in a gloomy, half-lit corridor swathed in hissing shadows. We could still hear the battle raging outside, but we already had our hands full here.

In a matter of moments, soldiers filed into the hallway on either side of us. I groaned under my breath. Of course, it wasn't going to be that easy. It never was. Frankie raised her hands, preparing to blast them. But before she could let off a shot, some of the ghosts melted through the walls. They split into two halves to block the soldiers. Dekala appeared, picking his teeth with a straw.

Eli cocked his head to the side. "I thought you said you wouldn't help us once we got inside the palace."

"I changed my mind," Dekala growled as he dodged a soldier, then tossed another one through a window.

The ghosts battled the soldiers as darkness fell over the corridor. The temperature dropped, and I clenched my teeth to keep them from chattering. Purple and black ribbons crawled up the walls and ceiling. They filled every crack and crevice, hissing and snapping at everyone in their path. These weren't the shadows that had possessed Sue at the Field Museum, or the shadows that attacked us in the forest. These shadows belonged to the man from my nightmares. I braced myself, my staff ready.

"Welcome, daughter of Elegguá," the Lord of Shadows said in his menacing voice. It came from all around us, like a weight bearing down on our shoulders. Some of the darkbringers cringed at their master's approach. I stumbled back, knowing one thing for sure. I couldn't let him catch me. "You are the key to my freedom."

No way, I thought, as I opened another gateway. We ran again and again, in and out of endless rooms, searching for my father's soul. I didn't know what it was supposed to look like, but I had to believe that I would recognize it.

Everything and everyone was a dizzying blur as I opened gateway after gateway. My legs gave out more than once, and Frankie and Eli helped me across the bridges of spinning god symbols. We'd only be in a room for mere minutes before soldiers or patrol officers rushed in to attack.

I almost dropped to my knees when we landed in a shadowed chamber with a glass coffin in the middle. Above it hung a glass orb suspended in the air by magic. Inside the orb was light threaded through with sparks of silver. It was Papa's soul. I could feel its warmth and familiarity, his laugh, and his stories all wrapped up inside it. I pushed back tears. We weren't done yet.

"Now," I said, and Eli tossed the staff to Frankie. She created a force field around the whole room to keep out the darkbringers. The symbols rearranged themselves on the staff, growing brighter. Thousands of them flew from the staff to reinforce Frankie's barrier.

I ran to the coffin, intending to use it to climb up to the orb, but I stumbled when I saw what was inside the glass. It was a sleeping girl who looked a lot like me.

TWENTY-NINE

HEY, THAT GIRL SORT OF LOOKS LIKE ME

SEEING A GIRL who looked like me in a glass coffin in the Crystal Palace was *next level* weird. She wasn't dead — that much was clear. The girl was lying on her back with her hands at her sides like someone straight out of a fairy tale. She wore furry slippers and a green dress that looked like leaves sewn together. Amber curls fanned out around her face. I noticed the points at the tips of her ears and how her brown skin had a golden hue that shimmered in the light.

Eleni reminded me of Nulan — the only other aziza I'd met. They had the same oval faces and high cheekbones. Sometimes it really sucked to be right, and this was one of those times. I'd thought that Eleni was helping the Lord of Shadows, but I never guessed that she was his prisoner. Had she been like this for a thousand years? I was relieved that she wasn't on his side, but this was worse.

"Whoa," Eli said, his eyes big and round. "She's pretty."

Frankie grimaced as she studied the glass coffin. "That looks like a stasis pod . . . to um, preserve her."

I shook my head, half in denial and half in disbelief. Papa believed that the Lord of Shadows killed his first family. He was going to be so upset when he found out that Eleni had been trapped in a box for a thousand years.

"We have to take her back." I pressed my palms against the glass. "We'll wake her first, then get Papa's soul."

"Maya, hold on, we don't know what might happen," Frankie warned.

I tried to pull away from the pod, but magic glued my hands to the glass. I could feel heat and energy fleeing my body. I squeezed my eyes shut, and I saw a sharp tear in the fabric of the world. It was a wave of immense energy with no mass, no dimension, almost invisible. I was in the chamber with my friends, but I was also at the center of the veil. It was like my mind had been split in two.

Layers of silvery light moved around me. It hummed with energy. *Buzz. Buzz. Bu. Bu. Buzz.* I picked up on an interruption in the hum that sounded like a hiccup. *Buzz. Buzz. Bu. Bu. Buzz.* Something was wrong with the veil.

"Help me," I heard a voice whisper. "Please."

I whirled around toward the voice, but then a sharp pain

ripped through my belly. At almost the same time, black lightning cut through the veil and the silvery light fell silent.

"No," I screamed, realizing what was happening. Flames spread across the veil, burning it away. And it was my fault.

The stasis pod was a much more powerful version of my staff. It was using my magic combined with Eleni's to tear the veil. Was this why the Lord of Shadows needed me alive? With Eleni's and my powers together, he could bring down the veil for good.

Eleni materialized in front of me. She had iridescent wings of blue, green, and gold just like Nulan. I was beginning to think that their resemblance wasn't a coincidence.

"Who are you, and what are you doing in my dream?" she asked.

"It's a long story," I said. Long, complicated, and a little awkward. "I'm Maya. I'm going to get you out of here."

Eleni frowned and rubbed her forehead. "It feels like I've been dreaming forever."

"You don't know the half of it," I moaned. "Can you wake yourself?"

"I've been trying, but it never works," she said. "My little brother is going to be so mad if I miss his first day of school."

Her words hit me square in the chest. She didn't know about her siblings or her mother. The Lord of Shadows would've taken her first and put her in stasis. I pushed back the tears threatening to break free. I had to hold it together if I was going to save her and Papa's soul.

"Take my hand," I said, trying to sound brave. "I'll see if I can wake you."

Eleni smiled as she reached out to me, but everything went black as soon as our hands touched. I blinked once, and Frankie's and Eli's faces came into focus. I was lying on the floor next to the pod, shaking, every muscle in my body on fire.

"What happened?" Frankie asked as they knelt beside me.

My head was swimming, and nothing felt quite real. I squeezed my eyes shut to fight back the dizziness. Tears trickled down my cheeks as I thought about Eleni, imprisoned her entire life for a mistake. The Lord of Shadows had tricked her. Now he was using her to start another war, maybe the final battle between the Dark and orishas.

"We're the key." I forced my eyes open. I couldn't hide from the situation. I had to face it. Frankie looked at the pod and me again, and then she frowned.

Eli looked back and forth between us. "What? I don't get it."

"Maya is the key to bringing down the veil," Frankie said.

From somewhere in a dark corner of the room came a slow clap. I jumped to my feet, even though it made me dizzier. Frankie gave me the staff to lean on.

Nulan melted out of the inky shadows. Zeran was with her in his regular form, no longer a copy of me. When I saw him walking in front of her, my heart dropped. He couldn't have betrayed us. He was our friend. But then I saw the bruises across his cheek and the metal collar around his neck to neutralize his magic.

"Congratulations, Maya," Nulan said, a faint smile on her lips. "You'll be spending the rest of your short life in this room beside your sister."

"You knew!" I spat, remembering when Nulan had taunted Papa about losing his family. "You knew she was alive and trapped here."

"Our lord killed the other two because they did not have Elegguá's ability to manipulate the veil." Nulan stared at the pod with a look of pity, then she shook her head like she was brushing off a memory. She was talking about my father's other children—Eleni's little brother, Genu, and her older sister, Kimala. "Look at her: a confused thirteen-year-old girl who was only trying to help her auntie."

"Lutanga was your sister?" I said, finally understanding why Eleni and Nulan favored each other. The realization of it and horrible truth hit me at once.

"She picked the wrong side." Nulan pushed Zeran so that he was next to us.

"I'm sorry," Zeran mouthed, his eyes sad. "I tried to get far away, but she caught me."

"It's okay," I said, then glared at the aziza. "It's not your fault that Nulan got her sister killed, along with countless other people."

"Enough talk," came another voice peeling from the shadows. His words pulsed in the walls as purple and black ribbons wriggled out of a corner of the chamber. First a few, then dozens, then hundreds.

I sucked in a short breath and held it so long that it burned my lungs. The Lord of Shadows glided from the dark as gracefully and deadly as a spider. He was every bit as frightening as I remembered, except he'd shrunk himself to a normal height. He was a head taller than Papa, with skin the color of the moon and violet eyes that glowed.

"This is a day of celebration," he said, his voice slippery. "I will finally put the world back to the way it should be."

I shook my head, clutching the staff hard. "I won't help you."

"Eleni didn't want to help me either, and look what happened to her." The Lord of Shadows glanced at the pod. He clutched his fist so hard that it shook. "I am so close after all these years. I will not let you stand in my way."

"How could you do this?" Zeran's eyes filled with tears. "We trusted you to protect our world, but you only want to start a war for petty revenge."

"Revenge is only petty to those who have no chance of exacting it," the Lord of Shadows hissed at him. "You are too young and idealistic to understand." Then he added after a pause, "You will be punished for helping the godlings. *Captain* Nulan will see to it."

Nulan's lips curled into a smug smile at the news of her promotion. She'd finally gotten what she wanted. "It would be my pleasure, my lord."

"I bet it would." Eli poked out his tongue at her. She growled. Then he turned to me and whispered, "I'm going to try something, okay? It's going to be weird."

"Don't do anything brave," I warned. Neither the Lord of Shadows or Nulan would hesitate to kill my friends. Now that the Lord of Shadows was so close to getting what he wanted, he'd be more dangerous than ever. But I was counting on his overconfidence.

"Your antics will not work this time." The Lord of Shadows laughed. "Captain Nulan, take care of the two godlings and the traitor."

"You know we have names, right?" Frankie said, speaking up. "I'm Frankie, and he's Eli. That's Zeran. We're people, okay? You don't get to hurt us to satisfy your personal goals—that's pretty shady."

"Shady or not," the Lord of Shadows snapped at her, clearly missing the point, "I am righting a great wrong."

"With another wrong," I said, "which means you're just as bad."

The Lord of Shadows recoiled as Dekala appeared at

Eli's side. He looked more ticked off than scared to see the ghost among the ranks of the undead. "You dare rise from your grave to challenge me again?"

"You don't get it, do you?" I said, stepping toward the Lord of Shadows. "None of us will ever stop fighting. We're not going to let you destroy either of our worlds."

"Are you sure?" Dekala asked Eli.

"Yup," Eli answered, and Dekala disappeared.

Frankie frowned. "I don't get it."

"I do," I said, remembering all the times that Eli talked about ghost possessions.

While the Lord of Shadows and Nulan focused on Eli, Frankie touched the collar around Zeran's neck. Sparks of electric current jumped from her fingers. Zeran cringed, gritting his teeth, but the lock cracked open on the collar. If he moved a muscle, it was going to fall off. I caught Zeran's eyes and looked between him and Nulan, hoping that he got my message. He winked at me.

"So, I have Dekala's power now." Eli flexed his fingers. "Telekinesis." He reached his hand toward the orb that contained my father's soul, and it dropped from the air.

"No," I said, but luckily the orb didn't break. It landed on the stasis pod, which had cracked a little. Eli might have Dekala's power, but he couldn't control it well yet.

Eli ducked his head. "Sorry—I was trying to get it for you."

Nulan launched to grab the soul, and I yelled, "Now!"

Taking my cue, Zeran flew straight into Nulan. They crashed and rolled on the floor. One of her magical blades materialized out of thin air, and she aimed it for Zeran's heart. But he was quicker. He pulled the collar from his neck and snapped it around Nulan's throat. Her blade instantly disappeared. *Captain* Nulan clawed at the collar right before Zeran head-butted her and knocked her out cold.

The Lord of Shadows advanced on Eli, but a third of his writhing ribbons froze in place.

"Nice try," Eli said, wagging his finger, "but I don't think so."

Frankie tried to add energy to hold back the other ribbons, but her magic was spent from the force field. Eli's nose started to bleed, and his whole body was shaking again. He wouldn't be able to hold Dekala's power long.

"Give me a boost," I yelled to Zeran. He knelt and let me use his clasped hands as a step to climb on top of the pod. I snatched up my father's soul, which was warm to the touch. Not wasting any time, I stuffed it in my backpack.

"Arghhh," the Lord of Shadows screamed as he bounded forward, ripping out the ribbons in Eli's grasp. His ribbons snapped around my ankle, and I hit the glass on top of the pod. Searing cold snaked up my leg. The lower half of my body fell still, and I couldn't move. I blinked, suddenly feeling tired—no, not tired, I was exhausted. My heartbeat slowed, and my eyes fluttered close. Why was I suddenly so sleepy? I forced my eyes open again and stared into Eleni's peaceful face, but I also saw a reflection of myself in the glass. My skin had turned ash gray. Oh crap. The Lord of Shadows was draining the life from me!

"I thought you needed me alive?" I asked, hoping to buy some time.

"You're mistaken," the Lord of Shadows said through gritted teeth. "I already got what I needed when you touched the amplifier the first time. It connected your powers with Eleni's long enough to permanently damage the veil. Even your father can't fix it now."

The amplifier? He meant the stasis pod. A hollow feeling spread across my chest as I puzzled out what he was saying. When I touched the pod, it had drawn my power into the veil. In that dreamscape with Eleni, I had a sharp pain in my belly; then, I saw the veil begin to burn along the edges where we stood. Because of me, the Lord of Shadows wasn't tearing the veil anymore. He was going to burn it down.

"No!" I kicked at the ribbons around my ankle. All I could think about was saving my sister and figuring out a way to reverse the damage to the veil. Miss Ida and the orisha council had been right about me—I had already made the same mistake as Eleni. I walked right into the Lord of Shadows' trap.

My staff sent streams of white light into the stasis pod. It cracked little by little until it gave. I rolled over just in time to not crush Eleni. The impact knocked the ribbons loose from my ankle. Now the Lord of Shadows glided toward me fast, his presence like a raging storm that would crush everything in his path.

I threw up my hand, and a gateway sparked to life in front of me. The Lord of Shadows tried to slow down, but he went straight through it and disappeared. I gasped, mostly in shock, as I closed the gateway.

"Maya, what did you do?" Eli asked. Dekala stood beside him again.

"I sent him to the bog," I said, breathing hard.

Dekala clicked his tongue and shook his head. "That won't keep him long."

"Help me with Eleni," I pleaded, desperate as I started to open another gateway. This one would get us back to the human world. This was much harder, and every second that passed, I could feel the Lord of Shadows drawing closer. He was already outside the palace gate when the new gateway sparked to life, revealing a black hole.

"Well, ghost buddy," Eli addressed Dekala, "it's been a lot of fun. Thanks for everything." He turned to help Frankie with Eleni, who was still fast asleep.

"You said you would free us, little mutant boy," Dekala protested.

Eli grinned as they lifted Eleni. "Oh yeah, I already did that back in the bog. You're free to find a new place to haunt."

Dekala looked stunned, then he broke into a wide smile. "You're okay, godling."

"Go," I yelled to my friends. "I'll hold off the Lord of Shadows."

Eli and Frankie carried Eleni and disappeared down the walkway of god symbols. I backed into the gateway, bringing up the rear.

Commander Rovey burst into the room. "Zeran," he yelled. "Stop her!"

"Where's Billu?" Zeran asked, tears streaking down his cheeks. "Where's my brother?"

"Safe from the shame you've brought on our family," Rovey answered, looking down his nose at Zeran. "There's no coming back if you help this godling escape."

Zeran dropped into a crouch. He looked back and forth between Commander Rovey and me. His hands trembled as he balled his hands into fists. "I'm sorry, Father."

Yikes—this was another awful revelation. I felt bad for Zeran, but we had to get out of here, and now. I grabbed his arm and jerked him inside the gateway as the Lord of Shadows burst through the doors of the chamber. Inky black bled across my vision as I slammed the gateway shut. Hundreds of clipped ribbons fell on our heads as the voice of the

Lord of Shadows echoed on the other side. *"I'll be seeing you soon, Maya."*

"Billu," Zeran whispered as I pulled him deeper into the gateway, which was collapsing behind us.

We caught up with Eli and Frankie, who were struggling to carry an unconscious Eleni. Zeran stepped in to help them as the gateway opened in the human world.

It was over for now, but the Lord of Shadows had what he wanted. I may have taken Eleni from him—and Papa's soul—but he was never going to give up. Eleni had opened the gateway that started the last war, but I had handed him the key to destroying the veil for good. Soon the Lord of Shadows would be free of his prison to wreak havoc on our world.

THIRTY

WE MAKE A SPLASH AT SCHOOL

THE GATEWAY SPAT us out in the hallway at Jackson Middle. Kids scattered out of our way, dropping notebooks, papers, and backpacks. They all gawked like we were aliens from outer space. Well, there was a blue boy with horns with an unconscious girl across his shoulder. A girl who didn't look quite human either. How did we land at Jackson Middle? I remembered concentrating on opening a gateway in front of my house. But then, I'd thought about what it would be like for Eleni to be at school with me. I must've gotten distracted.

"And that is how you enter a room," Eli said, not missing a beat. "Behold the League of Godlings and their dark-bringer companion."

"Who's the blue bro?" a girl whispered to her friends. "He's cute."

"He's got a tail," said another. "Whoa."

"Ms. Abeola." Principal Ollie pushed past a bunch of kids. This was not good. I was pretty sure we were in big trouble after leaving behind such a mess on our field trip. "Of all the irresponsible things to do—"

"What day is it?" I asked, desperate to know how much time we had lost.

"It's Monday morning," Principal Ollie answered, their awareness shifting from me to Zeran. Magic sparked against their skin. "No one's seen you three since Friday at the Field Museum, and we feared the worst."

For the first time since we met him, Zeran looked scared. He was by far the tallest boy in the hallway, but his shoulders hunched like he was trying to make himself small. Eli and Frankie moved in front of him in a protective stance, and I blocked Principal Ollie.

"He's with us," I said. "He helped us escape the Dark."

"You made it back alive." Winston spat. Candace and Tay were on his heels. He glared at me with narrowed eyes. "Thought you'd be in body bags."

"What's this Dark everyone's talking about?" Gail Galanis asked as she pushed through the crowd. She spotted us and stopped in her tracks. "Okay, this is officially the weirdest neighborhood I have ever lived in, and I've lived in a lot of weird places." She looked Zeran up and down, smirking. "So this is why you haven't finished your math workbook."

"Saving the world twice is serious business." I gave her a winning smile, and she actually smiled back.

"Did Eli say they were the League of Godlings?" Dion James asked a kid to his right. "That's so unoriginal."

"You have no clue what you're talking about." Eli projected his voice like a celebrity or something. "I'm the king of originality."

Principal Ollie's eyes shone bright with hope and concern. "Did you get it?"

"Yes," I said, feeling the presence of Papa's soul still in my backpack. "We need to get it to him now."

"Go," Principal Ollie said, but I was already opening a new gateway. "I'll deal with your infraction at the Field Museum later."

"You're still the biggest dorks at JMS," Winston hollered after us. This time we landed in front of my house. As soon as I stumbled out of the gateway, blue mist swirled around us until it became the cranky Johnston twins. They were back in their adult form.

"You three are in big trouble," Miss Ida announced, glaring at us. "What you did was dangerous."

I looked to Miss Lucille, who seemed to be holding her breath. "We got Papa's soul back."

"Hurry," Miss Ida said, her voice low. "He doesn't have much time."

Zeran stepped out of the gateway with Eleni still across his shoulder. Miss Lucille gasped, and even Miss Ida was blinking back tears now. Zeran looked between Frankie, Eli, and me, unsure of what he should do.

"Is that . . ." Miss Lucille's voice broke. "Eleni?"

"How is this possible?" Miss Ida whispered.

"She's alive." I pushed past the twins. "We'll explain later."

I ran up to the door, my legs aching. The apartment was dim inside with all the curtains drawn. Mama was nowhere in sight, but I knew where she'd be. I climbed the stairs two at a time to the second floor. Mama slept in the chair beside the bed, where Papa was still in a coma.

"Maya, is that you, honey?" She smiled, her eyes filling with tears. She came to her feet and pulled me against her chest. "I'm so glad you're home." She kissed the top of my head. "Are you all right?"

"I'm okay, Mama," I said, staring at Papa. "How's he?"

"He's . . ." Mama paused. "He's still here."

Her voice was so resigned, like she'd prepared herself for the worst. Papa was completely still. Unlike Eleni, his chest did not rise and fall. He wasn't breathing. His skin was chalky and gray, not its usual brown, and his locs looked withered. He was still glowing, but his light was weak. I could barely see it now.

I removed the soul from my backpack. The glass orb opened without trouble when I pulled the two sides apart. There it was—Papa's soul—a ball of spiraling light. I could feel the essence of his laughter, his joy, and his sadness in my hands. I walked over to the bed and placed the soul on his chest, not knowing where a soul resided in a body. And come to think of it, Papa's mortal form was a vessel either way. I held my breath, waiting for something to happen. The soul pulsed like a heartbeat, expanding and contracting, but it didn't join with his body.

"Is it too late?" I asked through sobs.

"No," Miss Ida said, slipping into the room with her sister. "Let us try."

Miss Lucille had healed our bruises after the darkbringers' first attack this summer. Now the twins waited for Mama's permission. She nodded as she wrapped an arm around my shoulders.

"Whatever happens, Maya," Mama said. "Your father would be proud of you."

She said "would be proud of you" like he was already gone. The cranky twins stood on either side of Papa's bed.

They moved in sync as they scooped up his soul. They both became swiveling blue mist as they pushed the soul into Papa's chest. It wasn't open-heart surgery or anything, but I still turned away, too afraid to watch.

Frankie and Eli stood in the doorway, both looking like they didn't know what to do with their hands. Zeran was behind them, staying in the hall.

Papa inhaled, and even the cranky twins jumped a little. I took a tentative step closer. Mama did too. Papa's eyes cracked open, and I covered my mouth to keep from squealing too loud. He was okay. He tried to sit up on his own, but the cranky twins helped brace his back against the headboard.

"Maya, baby girl, you saved my life," Papa moaned, his voice weak.

I squeezed his hand, which had turned back to its normal color. "The four of us saved you," I said, proudly glancing over at my friends.

Papa frowned. "Four?"

"I may have brought a, um . . . darkbringer back to the human world," I explained, thinking about how I'd have to tell him about Eleni next. "His name is Zeran, and he helped us rescue your soul and saved our butts a few times in the Dark."

Papa looked around the room, his eyes growing sharper. "Where is this Zeran?"

"That would be me." Zeran shuffled forward with his head down.

"It's been a long time since I met a darkbringer willing to stand up against the Lord of Shadows," Papa said. "Thank you."

"Excuse me for saying so, sir," Zeran interrupted him with a biting edge to his voice. "But you don't know us. Not everyone agrees with the Lord of Shadows, and many of us want to live in peace. I have a little brother back home. I don't want him to die in a war." Zeran bit his lip and glanced away.

I realized that he had spoken in English, not the darkbringer language. When we were in the Dark, we'd only understood the darkbringers because of the staff. Zeran had seemed confused when Frankie told him that we were speaking English, but he'd known our language this whole time. Somehow I didn't find that surprising—him being top in his class and all—but why had he tried to hide it?

Papa stared at Zeran, but he seemed to be seeing through him or thinking about something else. "Maya, you have to send him back. The human world isn't ready to know about the existence of other worlds."

"We can't send him back, Papa," I said. "The Lord of Shadows ordered Nulan to punish him. They'll put him in a metal collar to take away his powers and force him to do hard labor in the stocks."

Eli cleared his throat and spoke up. "Nulan will probably do worse to him. Zeran did headbutt her."

"It was an epic headbutt, too," Zeran added with a small smile. Once things calmed down, I was planning to talk to him. I couldn't imagine what he must be going through after leaving his brother behind and coming to a new world. Commander Rovey had done such a messed-up thing by locking his son up in a cage. That wasn't something you forgot or got over.

"Can't he hide in the human world in disguise?" Frankie asked. "He can change his appearance."

"He shouldn't have to do that," Mama said. "People need to know the truth. We can't keep pretending that there isn't another whole world that exists alongside our own."

"Whole *worlds*," I added, happy that Mama was on our side. "More than the Dark exists." I thought about all the doors to all the worlds that I could feel every time I opened a gateway.

"I'm not sure if I want to stay, but I can't go home," Zeran mumbled, staring at the floor. "My father won't want me back."

"It's not my decision to make." Papa let out a deep sigh. "We'll have to discuss this with the orisha council."

I resisted the urge to roll my eyes. I had nothing against the council, but they were too cautious with their decisions.

They wouldn't see things our way because Frankie, Eli, and I kept breaking their rules.

"We'll just have to convince them," I said, under my breath.

"Papa?" I heard a quiet voice from behind. My breath caught in my throat as I whirled around to see Eleni standing in the doorway. She had her arms crossed and was wearing my Oya purple sweatshirt over her gown made of leaves. I bit back a protest. Who told her she could wear my clothes? Also, why was she so tall? Not as tall as Frankie and Zeran, but much taller than me. Her golden-brown skin shimmered, and so did her amber curly hair. She was mesmerizing.

Tears sprang to Papa's eyes, and he stared at her like he was seeing a ghost. "Eleni." He wept. "Is that you, baby girl?"

A pang of jealousy cut through my belly. Papa called me that. She couldn't be his baby girl, too. Plus, she was older than me. I was the baby—well, *not baby,* but I was the youngest. Mama pulled me against her side. I was glad that we found Eleni and rescued her from the Dark, but that also meant that things would be different now.

Eleni crossed the room on shaky legs, which was quite a feat for someone who'd been asleep for a thousand years.

Frankie filled in the blanks in her usual matter-of-fact way. "We found her in a stasis pod in the Dark. The Lord of Shadows used it to amplify her powers to tear holes in the veil."

Eleni seemed to register the rest of us for the first time, and her golden eyes lingered on Mama and me. She opened her mouth to say something but decided against it at the last moment.

Papa was ugly crying now. Miss Ida and Miss Lucille were too. "Oh, Eleni, I'm so sorry," he said. "I didn't know. I thought you were . . ."

"I got a message from Auntie Tyana," Eleni explained through her sobs. "She said that she was going to help me save my friend — the little boy that I saw in the other dimension. I believed her." A fresh batch of tears sprang to Eleni's eyes. "Where's Mama, Kimala, and Genu?"

"They're . . . They're gone." Papa opened his arms to her, and Eleni fell into his embrace. She buried her face against his chest.

"Let's give them some privacy," Mama said, and we all filed out of the room. She was still holding on to me, even though I had smeared grime all over her clothes. "Miss Ida and Miss Lucille, can you take Eli and Frankie home? I'm sure their families will be happy to see that they're okay."

"It would be our pleasure," answered Miss Ida, her voice not cranky for once.

Eli shook his head. "*Tyana Nulan.* Hard to believe somebody that evil has a first name."

Leave it to him to crack a joke at a time like this, although he was right. In *Oya: Warrior Goddess,* the villains hardly ever had first names, including the notorious Dr. Z.

Zeran was doing that thing again, where he was making himself small so that no one would look at him. Mama smiled anyway. "Zeran, we'll set you up in our guest room until we can figure something out. Maya, you can share your room with Eleni for now."

"What?" I said through a grimace. "Can't she take the couch?"

"Not when you have a perfectly fine trundle you can pull from under your bed." Mama winked at me. "It'll be like a sleepover."

"Fun," I groaned. Things were about to get interesting around here.

THIRTY-ONE

WE GET A FRESH START (SORT OF)

I SLEPT IN LATE and woke up to Eleni digging through my closet. She was throwing my clothes over her shoulder onto the floor. I sucked in a deep breath, trying to keep from screaming at the top of my lungs. Who did this girl think she was, going through my stuff without asking? I cleared my throat to get her attention, but she ignored me and kept flinging clothes left and right.

"Um, hi," I said.

"Maya, yes?" Eleni spun to face me. Her voice was lyrical, and her words slid into each other like a song. She held up a blue pair of corduroy jeans. "Do you think these will be right for me?" She cocked one eyebrow. "They might be short, but according to the woman on the TV, ankle length is in style for this century."

"You've been watching TV?" I asked, scratching my head.

"Yes!" she said. "I was up all night with Papa. He showed me the wonders of the internet. The human world has come so far. It was so mundane before." Eleni turned to the mirror on the wall and pressed the pants against her waist. "They didn't have electricity and phones back in my time."

That sounded so weird coming from a girl barely older than me. I thought that Eleni was talking about all these things so she could avoid the hard stuff. She'd woken up from a thousand-year nap and found out that most of her family had died. The Lord of Shadows had faked being her friend, and her own auntie had helped trick her into opening the gateway. That was a lot to process. "Are you okay?"

Eleni stopped admiring herself and looked at me through the mirror with tears in her eyes. "No," she answered. "Your mother says that I'm in shock, but if that's true, why does my heart hurt so much?" She swiped at her eyes with the backs of her hands. "I can't stop thinking about how Kimala used to braid my hair and how Genu chased butterflies in our forest. Mama, she . . ." Her voice choked up. "I miss her singing and her smiles and her pudding."

"I'm sorry, Eleni," I said. I couldn't tell her that things would be okay, or that she'd get better. Sometimes people just needed you to listen to them — not try to solve their problems. I could do that, even if I couldn't do anything else.

"My father has a new family now," Eleni said, lifting her chin. "He has a new life without me, so where do I fit in this world?"

"I know this doesn't fix things, but you're not alone." I bit my lip. "You have me, Papa, and my Mama. We're your family now."

Eleni brushed tears from her cheeks. "You never answered my question about the pants."

"They're going to look good on you," I replied, raising an eyebrow. "That is until Mama takes you shopping for your own clothes."

"Oh, I already bought clothes online and got two-day shipping," Eleni said. "Apparently, you only need a credit card, and Papa's card was already saved on his laptop."

I swallowed hard, knowing that she was going to be in big trouble. Also, she'd learned how to use a laptop, the internet, and credit cards fast. "How much stuff did you buy?"

"Let me see." Eleni tilted her head to the side. "Ten dresses, a dozen pairs of jeans, twenty shirts, fourteen pairs of shoes . . ."

I zoned out after she got to bracelets and earrings. I fell flat on my back with a dramatic flair, feigning mental overload. She started to list out all the things she still wanted to buy.

"Let me get that for you," I heard Zeran's voice drifting in from the open window. I jumped out of bed and ran to see what he was doing. Was I the only one who decided to sleep in after everything we'd gone through in the Dark? Eleni and Zeran were making me look bad. No chance that Eli was already up, though. Frankie might be.

I didn't see Zeran, but another boy was helping the twins carry groceries up the steps to their greystone. The boy looked familiar. He was tall and lanky with curly hair. Wait a minute, that was Zeran looking like Lil Nas X. If I had to guess, the Johnston twins had already introduced him to the internet, too.

"Tell me, Zeran," Miss Ida said. "Do you like gardening? My sister and I win awards for our tulips every year."

"I have quite the green thumb," Zeran answered with a big grin.

"He'll be moving in with Ida and Lucille," Eleni told me. "Papa is going to let me have my own room, but I can stay here with you if you want."

"Oh, no, by all means," I said, rushing my words. "You should have your own room." I belly-flopped back on the bed. "I need more sleep."

"Who can think about sleep right now?" Eleni spun in a circle on her tiptoes. Her hair sparkled with light when she did. "We have a conference with the orisha council in an hour, and I don't know what to wear."

My heart fluttered against my chest. The council was going to be mad that we broke the rules again. Never mind that my friends and I put an end to the Lord of Shadows' evil plans for the second time in, like, three months. They were going to be *furious* when they found out that I helped set the veil on fire. "They don't waste any time, do they?"

"I'm not pleased about seeing them either." Eleni hugged the corduroys to her chest. "I messed up and started a war."

"First of all, you didn't start a war," I said. "The Lord of Shadows did that on his own, and second, I've got your back. The orisha council has to see reason. It wasn't your fault—the blame belongs to the person who actually is responsible."

Eleni flounced across the room like a butterfly and threw her arms around me. It caught me off-guard at first, so I seized up with my hands at my sides. I had always wanted a younger sibling, and now I had one almost my age. I didn't dare think we'd end up being best friends, but this was a nice start.

I hugged Eleni back, and she started to cry on my shoulder. I knew what it was like to make a mistake and to feel like I'd let everyone down. It was time for me to own up to my mistake, too—the one that sealed the fate of the human world.

***

The orisha council called an emergency meeting, and this time we didn't have an audience or bleachers. Mama and Papa brought Eleni and me. Frankie's moms, Pam and Dee, were with her, and Eli came with his little sister, Jayla. Miss Ida and Miss Lucille had stayed at home with Zeran to await the council's decision. We stood across from the orishas in the gods' realm. Shooting stars passed so close to the open chamber that they shook the floor. My knees shook, too, but that was for another reason.

Even after seeing this place a few times, I couldn't get over how wonderful it was. But I pushed that thought aside as the council members stared us down: Nana Buruku, Ogun, Eshu, Shangó, and Oshun. Well, scratch that. Ogun, the war god, and Shangó, the lightning god, were looking pretty smug.

"You children continue to break the rules that we put in place to keep you safe," Nana said after a deep sigh. Her eyes had dark circles underneath them, and she looked tired. "Furthermore, when asked to pledge your alliance to this council, you refused."

I opened my mouth to interrupt, but Frankie's mom Pam beat me to it. "With all due respect, Nana," she said, glancing at her wife, who nodded. Frankie stood between her moms with her chin up. "Dee and I aren't exactly happy that Frankie went back to the Dark, but we're proud of her. We're not going to deny her the opportunity to live up to her full potential. If she's meant to save the world, who are we to stop her?"

"This council does not deny the children their birth-right," Oshun, the goddess of beauty, chimed in. "We only want them to stay safe."

"These *children* stopped the veil from failing again," Mama reminded the council. "They put everything on the line to act while you're still waiting for the other celestials to arrive."

Okay, Real Talk. I didn't expect our parents to come into the gods' realm and go all the way off. Mama was wrong about the veil part, though. We brought Papa's soul back and rescued Eleni, but the veil was in a much worse state because of me.

"Some of us didn't sit around," Ogun said, stroking General's head. The dog howled at his feet, looking peeved at Mama's accusation. "We helped within the confines of our allegiance to this council."

"Be that as it may." Nana redirected the conversation. "We must hand down punishment for breaking the rules."

"Oh, come on, Nana," Eli whined, with Jayla clinging to his back. "Go easy on us. We did stop the Lord of Shadows for now."

"Yeah!" Jayla butted in. "Go easy!"

Nana sighed and rubbed her forehead. "These kids are going to be the death of me."

"They remind me of the fire you used to have back in

the day," Shangó said, which earned him a scowling look from Nana.

Eshu raised his hand in a truce. "Now, now, let's come to the point of this meeting before we get too far off topic. The council has voted to postpone deciding your punishments for disobeying our rules."

"Yes!" Eli said, turning a circle while Jayla bounced up and down.

Nana had that look—the one that told me that we hadn't heard the last of this. Our punishments would come, and they were going to be bad.

"For now, we must discuss the veil," Shangó said. "The other celestials will be in our solar system in a few months if all goes well."

"Which it never does," Frankie groaned under her breath.

"Elegguá, with you whole again, can you keep the veil up longer now that the Lord of Shadows can't use Eleni's magic?" asked Oshun.

Papa was already frowning, his forehead creased in deep thought. "That should be the case, but I sense that there is something else greatly wrong with the veil. It feels like brittle paper that could crumble at any moment."

"How could that be possible if Eleni's here with us?" Nana asked, leaning on the edge of her throne. "The Lord of Shadows shouldn't have a way to tear the veil anymore."

The room fell silent as everyone looked at each other in various states of resignation. War was coming between our world and the Dark, and we all knew it. I cleared my throat, and it echoed in the chamber as all eyes turned to me. It was now or never. I couldn't live with the secret of what had happened in the Dark. As much as I felt terrible that I let the Lord of Shadows trick me, I wasn't going to lie about it.

"I know why the veil is worse," I blurted out. I told them about the stasis pod — what the Lord of Shadows called an amplifier. How, when I touched it, the pod combined my magic with Eleni's to set the veil on fire.

"I remember a girl in my dreams," Eleni mused, her eyes wide. "That was you!"

I glanced down at my feet. "I'm sorry this happened — I was just trying to help."

"We tried to warn you, didn't we?" Oshun said in her high-pitched voice.

"Now is not the time, Oshun," Nana snapped at her, which surprised me.

I met Papa eyes, ashamed of my mistake. "The Lord of Shadows said we couldn't patch up the veil anymore because it was burning."

I expected him to be mad that I let the Lord of Shadows trick me, but he said, "You can't blame yourself, Maya. You did the right thing, but the Lord of Shadows continues to prove that he has no honor. To use children to fuel his war is a new low. Now that I know *how* he's making the veil brittle, I can see about figuring out if there is another way to stop it."

"And if you can't?" Nana asked.

"You already know the answer to that," Papa said, his voice heavy.

"I'll keep training the children," Ogun offered. "They'll need to know how to protect themselves and the humans."

Oshun tapped her long nails against her throne. "As for the matter of the darkbringer . . ."

"His name is Zeran," I reminded her in case she'd forgotten. "He helped rescue Papa's soul and free Eleni."

"Yes, we know," Oshun said. "Yet, we do not feel that humans are ready to know of another world. If he is to remain in this world, he must glamour his appearance. We can make it so that only godlings and orishas can see his true appearance, and humans will see him as one of them."

"We'll have to do the same for you, Eleni," Nana added.

"Um, I guess." Eleni frowned. I didn't think she was happy about hiding her wings. I wouldn't be either.

We weren't off the hook with the orisha council, but we had a little time before they handed out our punishments. I already knew that they were going to be brutal. No way the council would let my friends and me get away with breaking their rules yet again. Papa was better, and Zeran could stay in the human world. I would take any punishment they dished out to keep things that way.

The Lord of Shadows was still a threat, but I would train hard, and we would be ready for him when the veil finally failed.

THIRTY-TWO

The League of Godlings returns to school

I COULDN'T BELIEVE that it was only the second week of school. Zeran, Eleni, and I met up with Eli and Frankie on the way to Jackson Middle. Zeran was nervous about starting school with a bunch of strangers, but it didn't seem to bother Eleni. Also, to our horror, our parents had worked it out so that we could do catch-up work on the weekend at school. *Meh.*

Ms. Vanderbilt found it in her heart to give me another week to finish my math workbook. She thought I had taken sick, and that was why I had missed so many days in tutoring already. The Johnston twins made sure the human teachers and students had no clue about the godlings, but I didn't think that would work forever. Someone was going to slip up and get caught.

As we crossed Ashland Avenue, I looked up at the sky and saw thin vapors of gray smoke seeping through to our world. I tried not to worry, but I couldn't help it. Eleni saw it too, and she squeezed my hand as if to say that things would be okay. No, things wouldn't be okay—not for a long time.

"I've missed a year of school," Zeran said, pulling my attention back to the conversation.

"That's nothing," Eleni retorted. "I've been asleep for a thousand years, so I'm sure that I've forgotten everything."

"I can tell you that the way we do math changes about every two months," I grumbled.

"I can tutor you." Zeran clutched the straps of his backpack. "I'm pretty good at math."

Eli and Frankie exchanged a look, and Eleni laughed for no good reason. I frowned. "Why are you guys acting so weird?"

"Oh, no reason," Eli said. "Something's in the air."

The first day back at school passed in a flash. Kids came in groups to introduce themselves to Eleni and Zeran. They were instant hits, but we weren't the same dorks like Winston said we'd be. People were talking to us, too. They pitched their voices low so the human teachers wouldn't hear them asking about the Dark.

"Zeran, I really like your horns," said one boy.

"And your tail," added the girl with him.

"Um, thank you," he replied. "I like your . . . um . . . shoes."

He didn't specify which shoes he liked, but both kids blushed. I grabbed Zeran by his arm and pulled him away. "I'm sorry people are such a pain," I said. "They've never seen anyone like you before, but soon you'll be old news."

Zeran grinned. "I don't know if I want to be old news."

A lot of things still bothered me. Especially the last words the Lord of Shadows said: *I'll be seeing you soon, Maya.* The fact that there were darkbringer spies already in the human world. I couldn't help but think that I was missing something else.

We stopped in front of Zeran's locker, except Eleni got swept away by a group of godling girls admiring her wings. Miss Mae had glamoured her so that humans would see a normal girl, no wings, shimmering golden skin, or pointed ears. But godlings would see her true form.

There was a note crammed into Zeran's locker. Probably a love letter from one of his new admirers. Half the school wanted to be friends with him and Eleni. I shuddered at the thought.

Zeran read the message, and his jaw went slack.

"What does it say?" I teased. "Who's confessing their love for you?"

"It's nothing," Zeran said as he balled up the paper and tossed it into his locker. He slammed the door shut. But I could tell by the way he tried to play it off that whatever was in that letter was *not* good.

Winston stepped in our path with his friends at his side. Sparks of fire lit up on his arms. Candace grew to pro-wrestler size. Tay cracked his knuckles, and the floor shook beneath our feet. He'd finally found his godling power. Why did the universe have to be so unfair? I slapped my forehead. "Don't think because you have a new freak friend," Winston said, "you're not still number one on my hit list."

"News flash, Winston," I said, waving my arms, "we're on the same side."

Winston jabbed his finger into my chest. "We are not on the same side."

Zeran grabbed his hand and twisted. Winston fell to his knees, and Tay sprang into action. Frankie flung out an energy lasso that smacked Tay on his nose. He winced as he grabbed his face, looking annoyed. Candace tripped over Eli's invisible foot again, but this time she kept her balance. With the bullies disarmed, Zeran let go of Winston and shoved him back.

Principal Ollie bustled into the hallway. "My office, now! The whole lot of you."

"But Winston and his cronies started it again," I protested.

"March," they said, straightening their tie. "You know

the rules . . . no um . . . *horse-playing* in front of the other students." Translation: *No using magic around humans.* But the kids who weren't godlings didn't seem to notice anything amiss. They walked down the hall, chatting with their friends on the way to class. It wasn't like a few days ago when I opened a gateway at school. Some of the human students saw that, but Miss Ida and Miss Lucille had erased their memories.

We passed by Tisha Thomas, who leaned her back against a locker with her books hugged to her chest. She had an empty look in her eyes. "So many secrets and so many lies," she hissed. "He will betray you."

I followed her gaze to Zeran. He didn't seem to notice her as he strolled down the hall with the others. She couldn't have meant what I thought—that Zeran would betray me. I remembered when his father, Commander Rovey, told him to stop me from escaping. There was a moment that he had looked like he almost would. I realized something then that I hadn't put together before now. Captain Nulan. Commander Rovey. The darkbringer who could make illusions. The ones who'd snuck into the human world in disguises. The Lord of Shadows' real strength lay with the people who carried out his orders. Without them, he'd be powerless.

Zeran glanced back and smiled, and I could've sworn he had a dark gleam in his eyes. I pushed the thought out of my head. Tisha Thomas was wrong, wasn't she? Zeran wouldn't betray us, unless that was the plan from the moment we entered the Dark. Win our trust and undermine our efforts to stop the veil from failing. Distract and divide.

The Lord of Shadows was always two steps ahead of us, but had I unknowingly brought back a spy to our neighborhood? One who would do anything to help start a war? I cracked my knuckles as I trailed behind Zeran. I knew one thing for sure: the battle to stop the Lord of Shadows and save the human world was far from over.

ACKNOWLEDGMENTS

In *Maya and the Return of the Godlings,* our heroine has the support of her family, friends, and community throughout her journey. By the same token, I couldn't have written her story without the support, love, and encouragement from the people in my life. Always thankful to my mother, who read my first manuscript and called me up to rave about it to my absolute delight. Those early days of encouragement helped me get through the doubt and rejection that every writer faces. To my brothers, yes, I'll admit it, I'm the weird one in the family. There, I said it. Thanks for your love and support.

To Cyril for listening to me read random excerpts from *Maya and the Return of the Godlings* and my sporadic outbursts of laughter while writing. Thank you for your patience and your support during the ups and downs, both professionally and personally. You're there for the good writing days and the bad ones. Your dedication to your passion inspires me to never give up on my dream. When I'm so deep in the writing cave that I lose my way, you remind me to come up for air.

To my literary agent, Suzie Townsend, thank you for your encouragement and support. You are a tireless advocate and talented strategist, and I am thankful to have you on my team. Thanks to Joanna Volpe, New Leaf Literary Agency's fearless leader and mastermind. To Pouya Shahbazian, the best film agent in the known world and my go-to person for the latest on the best movies. To Veronica Grijalva, Victoria Henderson, and Mia Roman for shopping *Maya* in the international markets. To Meredith Barnes for your wealth of advice and strategy. To Dani, who is always on top of everything. To Hilary, Joe, Madhuri, Cassandra, and Kelsey, thank you for your support.

To my amazing editor, Emilia Rhodes at Houghton Mifflin Harcourt. I am always thankful for your thoughtfulness, sharp eyes, and support. I am lucky to have you in my corner. Thank you for giving me a platform to explore myself through these pages and tell a fun adventure story centering on Black kids, which I never saw when I was growing up.

I am so lucky to have a great team who supports *Maya*

at Houghton Mifflin Harcourt. Thank you to Zoe Del Mar for heading up marketing and Tara Shanahan for publicity. Your work is so key to making sure that people know about the book and getting it into young readers' hands. To Andrea Miller and the design team who came up with the amazing cover concept for *Maya*. To Elizabeth Agyemang, Mary Magrisso, Samantha Bertschmann, Ana Deboo, Annie Lubinsky, and Emily Andrukaitis. To Lisa DiSarro, Amanda Acevedo, Taylor McBroom, and the school and library team, I owe you my sincerest gratitude.

Again, so much respect to cover artist Geneva Bowers. You really brought Maya, Frankie, and Eli to life with your beautiful work.

To Mickey Mouse connoisseur Ronni Davis. You continue to amaze me with your energy, kindness, friendship, and humor. Thanks for being there for all the ups and downs and for introducing me to Sephora. It's always fun to talk about stories and characters with you, and a million other things.

To my ride-or-die friend and critique partner, Alexis Henderson. I am in awe of how incredibly talented you are. Thank you for your unrivaled support and our brainstorming sessions. Your enthusiasm and encouragement have been a lifeline.

To my writing family: Samira, Gloria, Lizzie, Ronni (hi again!), Reese, Mia, Lane, Rosaria, Ebony, Cathy, Nancy,

Irene, Nevien, and honorary members Anna and Kat. To the Speculators: David S., Antra, Nikki, Axie, David M., Nikki, Liz, Erin, Alex, Helen, and Amanda. You bring so much joy into the world. David Slayton, you are such an inspiration, and we would definitely have writing meetups if you didn't live so far away.

Thank you to the countless others who have offered me encouragement and support throughout the years.

The biggest thanks to the booksellers and librarians for championing *Maya and the Return of the Godlings*. And to the readers who've championed my books and sent me nice messages, thank you for everything. I owe so much to Mrs. Okeke. Her passion for literature helped me realize that a Black girl like me could tell stories too.